M000234349

Praise for *You or a Loved One*

"The stories in *You or a Loved One* explore the messy and complicated lives of characters from hardscrabble Florida and the bottom rungs of Louisiana, in the tangled devastation of the post-Katrina Gulf Coast. These characters are often one desperate decision beyond anything resembling normal. All of these lives are rendered with compassion and authenticity. There's an impressive array of types of stories in this collection; Gabriel Houck isn't afraid to experiment with form and structure, while always doing so in service to the story being told. What an impressive collection this is!"

–**David Haynes**, judge of The 2017 Orison Fiction Prize

"Gabriel Houck is a terrific young writer and this innovative collection shows off his intelligence, his humor, and his soulfulness; it's a diverse and entertaining inquiry into—as the author aptly puts it—'the meaning of our deeds and the truths of our hearts.'"

–**Jess Walter**, author of *We Live in Water*

"Gabriel Houck's stories are beautifully layered in ways that mirror the many choices and chances a character's life might offer while also focusing on their vulnerabilities. He has a great and insightful gift for locating those small moments and fragments of memory that bear the weight of a fragile life. One character says she is half of a lot of things, but not wholly anything; the stories in *You or a Loved One* are all about those complicated in-between and incomplete parts of life while also being very whole and satisfying. This is an accomplished debut by a very talented writer."

–**Jill McCorkle**, author of *Life After Life*

"Gabriel Houck's *You or a Loved One* is simply a stunning story collection. There's such grace on display in the prose, so much loving but clear-eyed attention to the lives of these characters. I can count on the fingers of one hand the number of times I've been so excited about a new writer. This guy's for real. Savor his work."

–**Steve Yarbrough**, author of *The Unmade World*

"The stories in *You or a Loved One* roll forward at an exhilarating pace, like a novel you read in an afternoon, propelled by a dynamite mix of comedy and tragedy, by the characters' heartbreak, their fierce skepticism, their warped perspectives. Houck's characters make me think of *A Confederacy of Dunces* and *The Horse's Mouth*—this book is right in line with those classics of comic tension and waggish portraits of delinquency."

–**Timothy Schaffert**, author of *The Swan Gondola*

"A stunning book of stories! I read it with growing exhilaration as Houck broke new ground in story after story, challenging our notions of history, reality, and imagination. This is the work of a terrific new voice we'll listen to for years."

–**Jonis Agee**, author of *The Bones of Paradise*

"Gabriel Houck's debut collection *You or a Loved One* is stunning: delicate and muscular, risky and tender, haunting and vulnerable—all at once. Wrenching, skilled, heartbreaking."

–**Joy Castro**, author of *How Winter Began*

You or a Loved One

You or a Loved One

Stories

by Gabriel Houck

You or a Loved One

ISBN: 978-0-9964397-8-7

Orison Books
PO Box 8385
Asheville, NC 28814
www.orisonbooks.com

Distributed to the trade by Itasca Books
1-800-901-3480 / orders@itascabooks.com

Cover art and design by Alyssa Barnes.

Manufactured in the U.S.A.

ORISON
BOOKS

Contents

Acknowledgments

Versions of some of these stories originally appeared in the following publications:

"You or a Loved One" in *Glimmer Train*, "Hero's Theater" in *Mid-American Review*, "Apocrypha" in *Western Humanities Review*, "What Distant Deeps" in *Grist*, "Al, Off the Grid" in *The Sewanee Review*, "Save Point" in *PANK*, "Reclamation" in *The Chattahoochee Review*, "When the Time Came" in *The Pinch*, "Homecoming" in *Moon City Review*, "The Dot Matrix" in *The Cimarron Review*, "The Refold" in *Bayou*, "The Wick" in *New Delta Review*, "Last Match Fires" in *Fiction Southeast*, "The Known Unknowns" in *Lunch Ticket*, "The Confession of Clementine" in *Sequestrum*, and "Missed Connections" in *Fourteen Hills*.

For Logan

You or a Loved One

We have this little flag we're supposed to raise above our cubicle when a real emergency comes in. It's a red triangle on a stick, maybe eight inches high, with *SaveLine* written on it. We're also supposed to ring the bell when we put the flag up, but most of us forget that step, or ring the bell at the wrong time, or ring it to annoy Raymond if he's hanging so close over our shoulders that we can smell him sweating through those weird plasticized dress shirts he wears. The flags started when Raymond made floor manager. I saw something like them once, at an all-you-can-eat Brazilian steakhouse back in Chicago. This was on a date, though that's an old-fashioned word for what it really was, and while the guy I was with had a system down—he'd keep the red flag up until prime rib appeared, then quickly raise a green flag and whistle—I remember marveling at how attuned all the waiters were to these little signals. Green for "don't stop feeding me," red for "don't stray too far." They had this topiary garden of a salad bar too, and we got so uncomfortably full that my date kept rolling down the windows on the drive home to pass gas. Later, with his dry fingers foraging between my legs, I remember imagining different hands, and then a carousel of men who were governed by little colored triangles that left nothing to chance, and that lost nothing in translation.

*

I got called a stuttering retard at work today, Kip says in his voicemail. His words are shaped so that I can picture his face when he says them, the way his eyes go half-lidded and his jowls sag when he's talking about something that hurts. My brother is a lonely man, but he isn't much of a phone-talker. Our routine is to miss each other, leave messages, and then listen to them on speakerphone while brushing our teeth or pulling whiskers or sorting the week's vitamins into pill-holders.

Kip's messages always begin with disclaimers—*Hey, Belle, it's me, no big agenda*—to show I shouldn't worry and that this is casual. Like many things with Kip, this posture means the opposite of what it suggests.

It's so unfair that they only have two of us in IT for an office of 150 lawyers.

I lay out a cowl-neck sweater for the weekend while his message plays. Tomorrow's work outfit hangs on the bathroom door, the grounds from the cold-drip coffee are draining in the sink.

Anyway, I wanted to quit when he said it. Another lawyer apologized for the guy, but it's not OK, you know? It's not OK, and I'm not gonna take it anymore.

Listening to Kip talk like this is hard. His thought process is an endless search for reasons to back out of things. He curates slights like a comic book collection, though in this case he also has a right to be upset. We have a poster of corporate etiquette taped to our breakroom wall that now and then gets defaced but is generally abided by within the office. The R word is definitely off limits.

I'm gonna go over to Mom and Dad's this weekend and talk to them about it.

Kip spends nearly all of his weekends at our parents' place back in New Orleans. I don't think he sleeps over, but he does laundry, helps Dad with rehabbing the deck or with grooming their jungle-garden. In the late afternoons he'll go for walks with them around the park or up to the levee to watch tanker ships chug upstream in the twilight.

Anyway, it is what it is. I love you, Sis . Give me a call tomorrow if you want.

I miss this outro because it's his standard closer, and because I'm starting to think the cowl-neck is too revealing for what I've got going on this weekend. Not that I'm entirely clear about what's going on. Nick texted cryptically that he has something important to talk about, something that requires we eat at a nice restaurant, and if ours was a bona fide relationship I might even have that hummingbird feeling in my gut because Nick's a confident guy, and there aren't many questions he would need a nice restaurant in order to ask. It irks me, though. It feels like some kind of setup. I want very much to find an outfit that says I'm not nervous—whatever the opposite of a woman with hummingbirds inside of her would wear. I sigh and delete Kip's message.

"It is what it is," I say to the sweater.

*

SaveLine costs customers $24.99 a month, with upgradeable packages for the grievously ill, homebound, or otherwise-friendless loners who don't want to twist an ankle and eventually be eaten by their cats. The upgrade customers (we rank these with gemstone coding—Ruby, Sapphire, and Diamond) are monitored in the same room as the regular customers, on a bank of computer screens flanking Raymond's office.

One of Raymond's first orders as floor manager was to do away with the practice of training the new hires on the upgrade banks. The upgrades are the only terminals that regularly signal real alerts, and until Raymond, the thinking was that it was better to have new hires get accustomed to being on their toes than get accustomed to doodling or posting restaurant reviews online, but Raymond is big on connecting the brand with the mission. Rubies, Sapphires, and Diamonds pay for a higher standard of care, he'd say. What if a Diamond in his high-rise condo has a heart attack and a new hire is slow to call the paramedics? What if the new hire hasn't yet mastered *the voice* (our proprietary, cop-nurse blend of concern and authority) and loses control of the situation?

As far as I know, none of this has ever happened, but changes were made. Now only three-year vets get to operate the Diamond controls. Two years for Sapphire, eleven months for Ruby. After Raymond first announced the new system, Ignacio leaned around our cubicle wall and whispered to me that rubies are actually worth more by weight than sapphires or diamonds. He said that his father was a jeweler in Bilbao, then he gave me a nervous, thin-lipped laugh like he was asking me permission to be in on the joke.

*

This morning I spent half-an-hour on the line with a woman in Spokane who said she'd heard a dog in her house, but that her own dog was dead and buried. It's been slow recently, so I stayed with her while she cleared the rooms, one-by-one. She said she had a steak knife just in case, which seemed appropriate, though as she huffed and gasped in my headset I began to picture scenarios where she would stab herself by accident and I'd have to raise my flag and ring the bell. After lots of listening, we determined there were squirrels in the bedroom walls.

With that mystery solved, she asked for my name so she could write SaveLine's HR and tell them what a good job I was doing. I told her I was sorry about her dog, and then suddenly she started to weep, with me right there on the line, these long slow moans with quick hisses between them. After a minute of this, Raymond cut in and asked me to stop by his office after lunch. I waited for a pause, then cleared my throat.

"I'm so sorry," I lied to her, "But I've got to go handle another call."

*

I lie all the time. I've chosen to live in a different city than my family so that I can lie to them. It's been true since college, and I've made my peace with this. My parents still think I'm a docent on weekends at the Walters and the BMA, that I'm serious about the professor who broke up with me five years ago, that I still submit my paintings to gallery shows around town. There are defensible measures of truth to each of these. Or, at least, at different times there were.

The truth now is that I'm half of a lot of things, but not wholly anything. I'm the quasi-girlfriend of a younger man. I'm a glorified switchboard operator, a knock-off grief counselor. I live alone in a quiet loft in Federal Hill, overlooking where the neck of the Patapsco River merges with the oily muck of Baltimore's Inner Harbor. I have no cats, though this doesn't keep Ignacio from gifting me *Hang in There Baby* posters and coffee mugs with whiskers on them for Christmas. I let myself go by degrees, smoke when I shouldn't, eat what I want. My window for children isn't entirely closed, but it already feels like a shuttered part of a shuttered house from which I've long since moved away.

What astounds me is not how disappointing this is, but how I've grown to need this solitude with the same certainty that I need caffeine in the morning and a noise-maker to sleep at night. I am strong enough to bear it, but my parents are not. They are in their 80s. And though they are young at heart, they have devoted themselves to the impossible task of building a safe harbor around my wayward brother. They are the coordinators of his days, the home-base from which he operates. They are his therapists, his priests, his advisors, and his best friends.

They allow themselves to be put on a pedestal so that he has something to work for; they are the purpose to his efforts in a world that so rarely offers him any other kind of reward.

This is their gift to Kip. The lies that hide my smallness are my gifts to them.

*

Raymond sometimes reminds me of the guy I've been dating. Raymond is taller than Nick, but what they have in common is that they're hand-talkers. No argument is complete without gesture, no order at a restaurant can be made without also indicating that choice on the menu. When I poke my head in to see what he wants, Raymond is cradling a phone on his shoulder and points me towards a chair, flattening his palm and lowering it like he's petting an invisible dog. I sit down. Because the windows in the manager's office overlook the call center, eyes from the main floor watch the secretary, and I space out while Raymond finishes his call.

With Nick, it used to be his hands that got me excited. They're long-fingered, dexterous, proportioned with the right amount of sinew and vein. Nick's younger than I am, and though I believe the distance between 25 and 40 isn't what it used to be, he genuinely seems to love that fact about us. No easy labels, each of us casual, each of us buoyed by the power of the other. His—and perhaps our—charm is in this sort of in-between-ness. Nick's a veteran of starchy boarding schools, of art colleges and NGOs. Each era of his life is stamped on the way he dresses, on the way he carries himself with equal comfort around hedge fund managers and pot dealers. He likes to ask about what I was like in my 20s, playfully filling in the gaps between the old and current me, as if I'm still a portrait being rendered and not already a print stamped in tin.

"Anabelle," Raymond says, loosening his belt to re-tuck his shirt, "*entrez vous*."

Raymond's dress code is a color-wheel of wrinkle-free dress shirts that slowly come untucked from his khakis throughout the day. I walk into his office and shake my head when he gestures at a pitcher of ice water.

"So we've been listening," he says.

"Listening."

"For quality-control purposes," he says. "Surely you're aware of this."

"*We* as in *you*, or *we* as in *the company*?"

"You were great with the lady in Spokane," he says. "I think you could've gotten away without the last comment about the dog, but she's a Lifer after that conversation, you know that?"

I smile and try not to watch his hands.

"From now on, she's going to think of us every time she gets indigestion after dinner or when she's short of breath on her walks. She may even live longer because she'll be less stressed about the 'what ifs,' because she knows that SaveLine and people like you are just a touch away."

"I appreciate that Raymond," I say, recognizing that I'm speaking in *the voice*.

"What's your secret?" Raymond asks. He places his hands against the space-age fabric on his chest. I open my mouth, but he isn't really asking me a question.

"Your secret is heart," he says. "It's all the more amazing because you're, you know"—he looks me up and down, his heart-hands uncurling and beginning to flutter —"unattached, in that, I mean, you know, *without children*, and yet, there's, so much, such heart."

I try and fail to imagine Nick speaking these words about the volume of my heart. Raymond's eyes have drifted, and I'm suddenly self-conscious of my appearance, less of the waddle and the hips than of the neutrality of my outfit, of the equation between 'professional' and 'childless' I've made with tan sweaters and roomy slacks.

"I need you with the Diamonds," Raymond says, his eyes back on mine.

"Is that a proposal?"

Raymond's face twitches, then he lets out a trickle of a laugh, finding his breath as he goes until he's laughing so loud that I'm sure the secretary can hear.

"Anabelle, we need your professionalism and compassion. We need your heart."

"I've only been here a year," I say.

"And technically that means you're only qualified for the Rubies," he says. "In this case, corporate wants to incentivize the performance of fast-track associates like yourself."

"When?"

"Immediately. Well, Monday, since we'll need the weekend to set up your terminal. But after today, you're a Diamond."

"Thank you," I say, and the clock ticks loudly for a few seconds.

"No, thank *you*," he says, his face serene, his palm swinging towards the door like a wayward high-five.

*

On the drive home, Kip doesn't answer my call. I leave him a message, omitting my promotion so as not to aggravate his mindset about work. Then I drive to the quiet hush of rain on the road, thinking about my brother.

Our parents sent Kip to a wilderness school when he was thirteen. It was in the summer, in southwest Colorado at the dusty edge of the San Juan Mountains, and he was too young by a mile. Camp brochures said ages 13-18, but Kip was still years away from the Asperger's diagnosis and the food counselor and the psychiatrist, and his little bird-framed body stood out, hobbit-like, in comparison to the other campers. He went because our father had a romance for Thoreau, for the rite of self-discovery in nature. He went because he wanted our father's vision of that passage to be real. He went because he hadn't learned—and never would—how to say no.

I spent that summer with our folks in Wyoming, on the ranch of a former English colleague of Dad's . It was more of an empty brick house in a field than a ranch, plastic seat-covers and Spartan army cots, but my father wrote his articles and my mother rode horses and I shot a bow and arrow until my left wrist was pink and tender from the strike of the bowstring. We all got chiggers from a picnic up in the hills. On the drive to Durango to pick up Kip, the car reeked of nail-polish remover and Mom's resurrected smoking habit.

It was a wet day when we arrived at the camp, with a low table of clouds clipping the peaks of the mountains and woodsmoke on the wind. We waited in a gazebo while a counselor fetched my brother, and I'll never forget the sound my mother made when Kip finally appeared. It was like a vowel that never found a word to fit into. It was like the airbrakes of a bus that sidles up and settles to a stop. She sort of dropped to one knee and just waited. Kip walked gingerly, as if on roller skates. When he hugged her, his emaciated frame disappeared into the fabric of her coat.

The head counselor took my father aside and talked about some things—about malnutrition, about what trenchfoot was and how to treat it. He mostly talked about how nobody knew anything until the end. About how they didn't see the eating disorder or the wet feet or any of it because Kip never spoke. Not once, for almost two months. The counselor said they'd never had so much bad weather on an expedition before, and that other campers took Kip's silence for stoicism and had mostly left him alone.

We drove away with a pulse in the car like we'd all been in a bad argument that had lasted for days. Dad would occasionally open his mouth but he didn't say anything. In the back of the station wagon, Kip slept the sleep of the dead. His face was thin and peaceful. I wrapped him in my jacket, and then rested my forehead on the window glass, picturing him at the back of a line of children that snaked through rain-shrouded mountains. A boy on skinless feet, as silent as our car the whole drive home.

*

There is a third place set at our table. When he sees me standing by the maître d', Nick gets up and flashes me a nervous smile, walking through a gold-lit cloud of tinkling piano music to kiss me delicately on the cheek. He's over-dressed for this restaurant, or maybe I'm under-dressed, but he makes a satisfied *hmmmm* noise in my ear after kissing me and fixes his eyes on the folds of my cowl-neck sweater once we're seated. His tie is matte black, his dress shirt is tailored, his collar is perfect. A waiter appears with wine Nick has already ordered, setting out three glasses and undoing the cork. Each time I open my mouth to speak, he holds a long finger up to his lips, his eyes glittering.

I've already started thinking about it when she appears from the women's bathroom. Not in the way that Nick surely wants me to have guessed, but more generally, I am thinking about what this is and what it says about us that he thinks I would be disarmed by this kind of intrigue. I can't quite believe it, but I find that

I am already making excuses for him. I'm picturing myself in the gray glass of Nick's eyes, someone who was a senior in high school when he was still in diapers, someone who since then has *settled* in nearly every sense of the word. In fairness, how could things have gone on this long before he decided he'd had enough?

"Belle, this is Melissa," Nick begins. "And before you say anything, the answer is no, we're not having an affair."

Melissa is wearing a contour dress the color of champagne. She is young and tall and milk-skinned, with swimmer's shoulders that I'd swear are broader than Nick's. She flashes a sheepish smile, her teeth glowing in the low light.

"Nick told me this was a surprise for you," Melissa says. Her voice is soft, vaguely southern. "I'm sorry for that."

Nick's smile levels out a bit, and they exchange glances.

"And I promise that he's not lying," Melissa says. "We haven't even held hands yet."

Yet. I laugh, a kind of hoarse croak, and this shuts everyone up for a moment. I take a long, steady drink of wine, watching the shapes of Nick and Melissa wobble through the rim of the glass.

"Well you're right," I say, my glass still raised like a toast, "this is certainly a surprise."

Nobody seems to want to be the next one to speak. A waiter glides up to the table with bread, places the basket gingerly between the three of us, hovers as if he's waiting for us to approve.

"Did you know that Nick's money isn't really his?" I ask Melissa after finishing my wine. The waiter stiffens, then glides backwards and away.

"His father is a free agent for white collar criminals, and his mother is an heiress," I continue. I'm less surprised by what I'm saying than by the flatness of my words. I sound like I'm reading a script, like I'm doing *the voice*. "I don't think he even paid for that tie."

"Belle—"

"Though if he wanted to break up with me I don't see why he'd need an escort to do it."

Nick groans. A girl at the hostess stand laughs.

"I'm . . . an account executive at Nick's studio," Melissa says after a pause.

Nick's hands are doing a little dance, organizing the silverware in front of him and then pressing the lines of his napkin. He keeps looking back and forth between me and Melissa, and though I still don't really know what's going on, I'm also feeling something unravel, a floaty sensation, like I'd already finished the bottle of wine.

"I think we're on the wrong foot here," Nick mumbles into his napkin, "definitely the wrong foot."

"We met at the Christmas party last year," Melissa says, ignoring him. "And Nick wasn't going tell you this part, but I can tell that we've offended you so I really want you to know this. He gave me a ride home after. I wanted to sleep with him but he wouldn't do it. He told me all about you instead."

"Congratulations," I say to Nick. The floaty feeling has pulled me above a fire that kindled when Melissa first appeared.

"We've stayed friends. Or I guess you could say we're friends because of it, if that makes any sense, and –" here she looks over at Nick, whose face is a mask, his eyes almost closed and his hands still—"he told me your anniversary was coming up, that you were into new things, and that maybe we, well, the three of us, you know, only if you were interested of course . . . "

She keeps talking, but I'm drifting now, a slow bird's-eye tour of the restaurant, of its crystalline snowball tables and candle glow and hushed waterfall of chatter. I wonder what day it is. I wonder if it really has been a year since Nick and I met, what the weather was like outside on our first date. Whether we even had a first date. Time passes in a strange way, because soon the bread is gone, and then Nick is ushering Melissa away from the table, and the gliding waiter is removing our glasses, and I recognize, with something that feels like relief, that I just don't care.

*

There was a poem, written by Kip's namesake, that our father used to read to us at night. There were several poems, though Kip's favorites were the ones where our father would do the accents and the voices—*So ere's to you, Fuzzy Wuzzy, at your 'ome on the Soudan!*—with a roll of his shoulders and a pouty grin. Kip sometimes mouthed the words he knew, or smiled at Dad's voice, though he'd be asleep long before the poems were over. My brother could fall asleep like a light switch. Once Kip was out, Dad would shift to a voice he used with his college students, this soft and rounded baritone that always made me think of kitchen stoves in winter. He'd read from a wicker chair in the middle of our room by the glow of an orange-shaded lamp pulled up to his shoulder. He'd slow down, pausing for police sirens and for the distant bellow of tugboats that drifted in from the river.

In the last year before Kip and I started sleeping in our own rooms, dad would always finish with the same poem. He'd read others besides Kipling—David Young, Robert Graves, Wilfred Owen—but he'd always circle back at the end. I'm ashamed now to have forgotten so much about it. It was about a lost path through a forest, green beyond green, and wet with the breath of hidden things. Doves and badgers and otters would chatter in the trees, though in my mind's eye, they'd grow quiet when I passed, only speaking again once I'd moved on, even though I'd strain on tiptoe to catch pieces of their words trailing behind me. By the end of the poem, my father would read only in a whisper.

But there is no road through the woods, he'd say. Then he'd breathe a long, quiet breath, and click off the light.

⋆

The first thing I do after leaving the restaurant is block Nick's number. My brother calls five times over the remainder of the weekend, but I can't ever bring myself to answer. I drink the contents of my liquor cabinet in the dark, watching the lights of the harbor smear themselves across the black water, waiting for the buzz of voicemails that strangely never come. Five calls, no messages. Finally, on Sunday night, as I sink into the folds of my bed like a corpse into a grave, a last text from Kip: *I love you Belle, just so you know*. The words sit there, throbbing, sounding a little more alarming each time I read them, but by the time I try to dial him back I am already dreaming.

⋆

The overnight skeleton crew is still brewing coffee when I arrive Monday morning. Through the windows, the first rays of sunlight graze the peaks of the downtown high-rises. Raymond, his waxy shirt glowing electric blue under halogen lights, gives me a little golf clap when he exits the elevator a few minutes before seven. *Now that's what I like to see* he says with a grin, his hands clasped together afterward as if in prayer.

The Diamond terminals don't have flags or bells. We have a direct line to emergency services built-in, and there is even a chat window linked to a company-retained medical consultant meant to advise us on ambiguous symptomology. I kind of miss the low-tech flags and cubicles at first, but the consultant comes in handy. A different standard of care, Raymond had called it. A sleeker computer screen. A gold-embossed nameplate. Advice on the difference between gas pain and appendicitis.

By lunchtime, my adrenaline is gone. I can smell the ghost of liquor in my sweat, and I'm clock-watching my way through the minutes while snippets of Saturday's dinner pop up like unhappy Polaroids in my head. I've already sent three calls directly to EMS, each of them labeled *non-contact*, meaning the client had hit their panic button and didn't respond to calls made to their phone or SaveLine device. More often than not, these end poorly.

I remember the uncertain weight of Nick's hand on my shoulder when he left the restaurant, but I can't quite picture him.

A man calls in with chest pains, spacing out his words one at a time while we wait together for an ambulance. Later, he forgets to switch off his device, and I spend a few minutes looking up how to remotely disable it while listening to paramedics work on him in the background.

I keep thinking of that untethered sensation I felt at the dinner table, of the way suddenly nothing had seemed to matter. I find myself wishing it would return to me right now. I get a caller from Tucson who says he's flushed his medication because the federal government is poisoning it. Then another from Idaho who is trapped in a parking garage. Then another *no-contact*. I am exhausted by their need. I resent them for it.

⋆

The last call comes at exactly six. It's a younger voice, a man, distraught and muffled, as if he's unable to speak directly into the device.

"It's my boss," he's saying, "I think he's having a heart attack."

I ask if he's calling on his boss's device and the man says yes, his voice watery. I ask him if someone has called 911 and he says he doesn't know.

"We're locked in the bathroom of his suite," the man says, "I'm not sure if he's breathing."

"I'm calling paramedics now," I say, hitting the direct line to EMS, "can you get him on a flat surface? Is someone else there to help you?"

"We're locked in," he says. "One of the guys downstairs just went crazy a few minutes ago. I think he's got a gun."

For a moment I don't know what to say. Dread starts to percolate in my gut.

"Someone has a gun?" I say.

"Downstairs in the office, we hid in here."

I switch over to EMS and tell them law enforcement is required.

"Do you have aspirin on you?" I say, switching back.

"Oh Jesus Christ Jesus I can still hear him out there," the man says. Beyond his voice there is a warble of noise, distant shouting. EMS comes back that law enforcement is already notified and is on scene.

"Sir, help is almost there. I'm going to walk you through CPR, okay?"

There is a popping sound on the line.

"Jesus, Jesus, please don't leave," he says.

In my pocket, my phone vibrates. It feels like my peripheral vision is starting to gray out, like the evening fogs that drift in from the water.

"First, you're going to check his airway, then lay him flat on his back," I say, though I've lost the ability to hear myself outside of my own head.

"Ok he's on his back."

More popping sounds in the background.

The man's breath is like the rusty hinge of a seesaw.

There is a buzzing in my pocket again. It is the long single tone of a voicemail. I wonder if it is Kip, and the moment I think this, something strange happens. The voice of the man on the line somehow becomes my brother's, as clear as if I'm hearing it for the first time. I can see his jowls sagging, his shoulders hunched, his eyes on the middle-distance as he speaks. I am trying to talk to him but he won't stop interrupting, even as my own voice gets fainter.

"Please tell them to hurry," he says.

My brother is far off. He is climbing, out of earshot, disappearing into a curling tongue of clouds.

"Please tell me what to do."

He knows there are no safe harbors.

"Please don't leave."

There is no road through the woods.

"*Please.*"

After the line goes dead, I feel the fabric of Raymond's shirt against my cheek. I feel the weight of my body being carried through patches of air-conditioning and sunlight. I do not see the faces crowded around. I do not see the news bulletin flashing on the break room television, or the secretary who keeps pressing a water bottle to my lips and spilling it down my cheek. What I see is my father's face. It is cut in half by shadows from the orange-shaded lamp. He is utterly still, his eyes on Kip's tiny, sleeping chest as it rises and falls, his own features frozen like he might stay in that spot forever, or for as long as he can, or for as long as it takes, if only that were long enough.

The Dot Matrix

1.

It took a while for word to reach me that Casey Graham had printed images of naked women on his stepfather's dot matrix and was selling them for a quarter behind the backstop during recess. I'd spent that recess the way I always did—by the tetherball, arguing with Kendall Charbonneau about what goblins ate when they weren't eating humans. By the time Kendall and I arrived, Casey was already putting his things away, his pockets fat and jangling. Heat bloomed from the dirt by his feet. Casey had left the strips with the little holes on each side of the paper, and he'd scrawled girls' names on the top corner in tight, purple cursive: *Brittany. Roxanne. Delilah.* Around us, kids admired their purchases.

When it was clear to me that there were no more pictures for sale, I pushed Kendall hard to the ground and told him he smelled like baloney sandwiches. The only thing more shameful than not getting a naked-lady picture was appearing to want one and missing out. Kendall struggled to his feet gamely and called me a fucker. Casey winked at us as he walked by, the clink of quarters marking his steps across the sun-dappled courtyard. We kept up the performance until Casey was out of earshot and then turned together, still holding each other's shirts, to watch him disappear like a mirage through the junior high stairwell towards the vending machines.

2.

During math class I sat by the windows. Out in the yard, Mr. Alphonse and the recess chaperones smoked cigarettes and examined the discarded hole-punch strips curiously. I watched Mr. Claiborne waddle around the kickball diamond in a half-hunch, scooping paper bits from the dirt, fingering the mangled pieces with great concentration. Mrs. LeBlanc sniffed one strip and then glanced around to see if any of the other chaperones were looking. Mr. Alphonse's caterpillar eyebrows were furrowed as he scanned the yard. Then he glanced up and caught my face in the window. I leaned back into my seat, hoping to fade from view. I imagined a cloud bank overtaking our classroom, that the AC fog on the glass had hidden me, and turning back to the list of algebra problems on the board, I imagined that Mr. Alphonse would suck his teeth and wonder whose face he'd seen in the window, and, after another cigarette, whether he'd seen a face at all.

3.

One of the many ways in which Father Son and Holy Ghost Episcopal was a small-scale replica of our New Orleans suburb was that nobody in middle school had locks on their lockers. The junior high kids started getting combination locks after Fat Travis and the twins clogged a storm drain with the 8th graders' stolen athletic shorts. Father Richardson delivered a scolding about it at morning chapel, but most of us saw the theft as the coolest thing Fat Travis had ever done. Kids who otherwise made fun of how those tiny shorts clung to his dough-bulge thighs gave him knowing nods in the halls, a fist bump now and then in recognition of a respectable act of sabotage. Not long after, the twins were elected to student government on the platform of monthly pizza lunches and a proposal to allow students to bring their own athletic clothing to gym class. We got the pizza lunches, but the gym uniform issue must have died in committee.

4.

Everything at Father Son was governed by alphabetical order, so Casey Graham's locker was in the third floor hall by the bathroom, one down from mine. We were bonded by the first letter of our surnames, forced to be aware of each other's absences and to sit in mismatched proximity in the classes we shared. Our assemblies were a social-status checkerboard, *popular, nerd, follower, nosepicker*, all of us lined up in polos and khakis against the stiff-backed pews of chapel, and while I was definitely a nerd, Casey wasn't so much popular as he was someone that girls were interested in. He'd grown into his body proportionally, and in a class of puppy-legged weirdos and squeaky-voiced dungeon masters, that's all it took. He almost never spoke to me. It hurt to be ignored, but I never spoke to him either. Instead, I spent these assemblies entertaining secret hopes for a new kid with a G name to join our grade, someone just cool enough to bridge the transition between us, someone to shuffle up the checkerboard.

5.

The day after Casey's printer-porn fire sale, I'd been brooding on a plan. When ten sleepy minutes of 5th period study hall had passed, I took a deep breath and asked to use the bathroom. Ms. Hester smiled and handed me a battered cowbell with *Hall Pass* stenciled on its side. Ms. Hester was blonde, single, and the star of many unspeakable recess fantasies, and any other boy would've taken that smile all the way to the bathroom, but I was nervous. When I reached the stairwell, I held the clapper so the bell wouldn't rattle, and took the stairs two at a time. The third floor only had Geography in the afternoons, and from a classroom down the hall I heard the tinny sounds of an orchestra and a British voice say *Iceland gives us a view of the fires of creation.*

Casey's locker was a rat's nest of clutter, topped with a Cannibal Corpse T-shirt he liked to wear after school. Beneath the shirt was his backpack, and I felt a tightness in my lungs as I rifled through his things, resisting the impulse to linger on odd finds—medicine bottles, novelty pens, several uneaten bags of seaweed chips that lay crushed beneath his textbooks. I opened a folder with the words GROUP PROJECT on the cover, and inside, as I'd hoped, there were more naked prints. I thumbed through them, trying to organize dot-shaded images into recognizable shapes. I made out some faces. A tit here and there. Most were like magic-eye puzzles, these shifting cloud-animals of sexy potential that made me strangely uncertain. When I switched the folder over to my locker, I felt, momentarily, as if I were somehow even more deeply unenlightened, once again the last to be let in on some big secret, fumbling along with goddamn Kendall Charbonneau in a plot that Father Richardson would surely condemn in morning chapel if it weren't also so silly and pathetic. *Yet the story of our creation is also a story of destruction,* said the British voice from behind the classroom door.

6.

I made Kendall two bets and almost won them both. He didn't think I'd have the balls to steal Casey's pictures, and he didn't think I'd be able to get away with it. I'd surprised myself on the first bet. After the heist, I spent the rest of study hall feeling like I'd swallowed glowing coals, and I tried to focus on the smooth curve of Ms. Hester's clavicle where it emerged in wishbone symmetry from her wide-necked sweater. Kendall wanted to see the pictures on the bus that afternoon, but I had no intention of taking out the folder again until I was safe. He pouted, even threatened to tell on me when the bus approached our stop. Kendall wasn't a coward—I'd seen him drink a milk carton filled with condiments on a bet—but I knew he wasn't going to tell on me. I was his only real friend, and he wouldn't jeopardize this, even for a chance to look at dot matrix lady parts. I promised him that we'd look at the pictures together soon. I would sleep over at his house on Friday and we'd each get to choose and keep our top three favorites. He smiled at this, licking his fingers and then pushing his golden bangs off his brow.

"I'm going to name my top pick Angela," he said.

I watched the Mississippi River slide past us through the grease-smudged windows of the bus. "He already wrote names on them," I said. "You saw it yesterday."

"So what," Kendall said, his eyes on the water. Maybe he had a point, but I forced a dismissive laugh anyway, the kind I'd been practicing in the mirror at night as if I'd remembered lots of funny jokes while brushing my teeth. I thought about Ms. Hester and the grayscale shading at the edge of that sweater, about the mysterious dots and lines beneath it. I wondered what her first name was, and beneath us, the asphalt hummed.

7.

Nobody mentioned the theft the next day at school. There were no summons to the headmaster's office. I wagered that it wasn't in Casey's nature to complain to a teacher, and in this case, that he'd have to fess up about what was missing if he did. Being right about this buoyed me with such confidence that when I found him at lunch, I went right up and asked if he'd brought more pictures to sell.

"Why don't you and Tubby go kill some goblins," he said, stashing a bag of seaweed chips into his backpack. "Maybe one of them has some nude pictures."

My stomach made a whalesong moan that prompted giggles from the girls. Casey stared at me. It felt like I was being examined by a grownup, a man forced into an undignified pastel polo shirt and church pants, but a citizen of a broader world I knew instinctively I'd never seen. I wondered for a moment what Cannibal Corpse's music sounded like.

"I'm fucking with you," he said. Over his shoulder I saw Kendall watching me from our table by the lower school's Easter dioramas. "My stepdad's modem broke is all. Come find me Monday at recess."

"So you get them from the internet?" I asked. The question sounded so naïve that it hurt to hear it spoken aloud, but Casey leaned in.

"My stepdad now subscribes to Hustler online," he said. "He'd catch me if I swiped his magazines, but with this I can print them and nobody knows anything." He grinned clean, white teeth.

"How long does it take for you do that?" I asked.

Casey shrugged, and I imagined the anxiety of outlasting the *screeee haaaaaaa* of the dialup, the plodding whine of the dot matrix printing a pair of tits line-by-excruciating-line. I watched his eyes, gold-grey starbursts gilding the deep well of his pupils. I wondered if he knew that I knew he was lying about the modem and the missing pictures, and I wondered if he knew how small I felt for not calling him out on it.

"My parents got one of those ethernet connections," I lied. My cheeks flushed, but I was thrilled instead of embarrassed by this ridiculous falsehood. I watched Casey's pupils widen. I felt seductive, and behind the rush of blood in my ears the beginnings of what felt like a plan were fitting together in my mind, little sandwich layers stacking up towards a grand feast. Back at my table, Kendall was swordfighting with juice box straws.

"If you want you can use it sometime."

8.

"It doesn't matter what the goblins are eating," I said through a mouthful of instant mac 'n' cheese, "they're in the room when your characters show up. They're hideous. One of them has a battle axe that does extra damage to elves. That's what matters."

Kendall sighed and fiddled with a figurine from the formation laid out on his carpet. I was the Dungeon Master. We were in pajamas, and from the living room we could hear his father watching television, some cop show where the censor-beeps chirped and warbled like a broken fire alarm.

"Well, describe them some more," he said.

"They're in matching chain mail. The one with the battle axe is bigger than the rest, probably their sergeant or something. They shout when you open the door, and all of them move in to attack."

"How can I tell that the big one's battle axe does extra damage to elves?"

"It's enchanted."

"How do I know that?"

"Because it glows red," I said angrily, sensing Kendall flinch. Beeps and boops sounded from beyond the bedroom door. He repositioned his character figures on the floor, studying the crude map I'd drawn for him on a pad of looseleaf between us.

"So there's just three goblins living behind a locked door in this ancient tomb," he said.

I nodded, doodling on my notepad.

"I wonder how they got past the pitfall that killed Giganticus," he said, petting a figurine that lay on its side on a piece of paper marked *GRAVEYARD*. I let the question settle in the room without answering him. "Maybe there's another entrance they use," he mumbled.

"Maybe," I said.

9.

A few years before, when I was in fourth grade, my uncle took me sailing on one of the ponds scattered around his summer home on Cape Cod. It was cold for summer, and chilly foam spat across the bow of our boat as we chunked through the waves. My uncle was a pragmatic man, and not someone particularly interested in the fantasies of a ten-year-old. He told me what ropes to hold, when to duck the boom, but he could sense that my mind was elsewhere, and he watched my lips move as I scanned the water and practiced the names of sea monsters.

"Do they teach logic at that school of yours?" he asked me.

I wasn't sure how to respond. Even back then I knew that my uncle had a cruel streak, a bloodhound sense for difference and for weakness, and everything about his question felt like a trap.

"Logic," he continued, "as in: all people are X, and you're a person, so you're X?"

"Like math?"

My uncle swung the bow towards the shoreline, and a rainy mist began to prickle the skin of the water. He pointed to a stand of pines by the inlet.

"If one of those trees falls," he said, "and you're not around to hear it, does it make a sound?"

"Of course," I said, and I could tell immediately I'd given him the answer he wanted.

"But how do you know?" he said with mock astonishment, "If you weren't there to witness it, how do you know what happened?"

I didn't answer, but later that night I squirmed in bed at the uncertainty he'd seeded. What felt so insidious was that the idea was proposed by a grownup, by a veteran of the truths of the adult realm. What did he know that I didn't? Images played in my mind: shoes that moved in the dark while I slept, closet doors that waited for a room to be empty before opening. My imagination married into this uncertainty so seamlessly that I spent the rest of that summer haunted by the empty spaces I'd just left, and by the rooms I was slow to enter.

Things got so bad that my parents had me see a therapist that fall. We talked about the known and the imaginary. We talked about belief. We did exercises. Over time I became more and more ashamed, and my anxiety didn't lose its power. Instead, I learned to squelch it with just enough confidence to try standing in a dark room alone as the therapist suggested, to count to ten and then expect things to be where I'd left them when the lights came back on. I learned, much to my parents' delight, another step in the complicated dance of passing for normal, and with it a shaky faith in the realness of things, in the basic facts of the world

.

10.

Kendall named all three of his pictures Angela. He scratched out purple cursive and wrote A-N-G-E-L-A wherever there was white space left on his pages. Selecting our pictures lasted over an hour, much longer than our D&D game. I could see the shapes of his women as we made our beds, two with their legs spread in the air and one on her knees with a hand resting cockily on her hips. None of it seemed very sexy. After lights out, I lay in my sleeping bag and watched the lights of passing cars play across the ceiling of Kendall's room. I listened to him masturbating. I could hear the sheets moving, hear his puffs of breath when the AC clicked off. My sleeping bag had a plasticized coating that swished when I moved, so I squeezed myself firmly in one hand and played my fingers over the stack of printer pages scattered around the floor. I tried to connect the dots from the pictures I'd coveted, to arrange them into a woman willing to reveal herself to me. I tried to picture Ms. Hester, the mystery beneath her sweaters, the coy turn of her lips when she asked us to be quiet. I wanted to hear her say something, anything, but all I heard was Kendall breathing, and when I came I saw not Ms. Hester, but grey eyes flecked with gold, watching me grope in the dark for stolen pictures, pitying me and forgiving me all at once.

11.

My parents didn't get an Ethernet connection. I begged all weekend. I promised twice the chores, even to pay for it out of my allowance. The plan to get Casey to come over to my house was unravelling, but the more I insisted the more skeptical my parents became. I even pretended that Ms. Hester had recommended that students get faster internet access at home for learning purposes. I found myself shouting at them through my bedroom door that I'd have her write a note, that even the school computer lab had Ethernet, that my grades would suffer if I weren't able to research things at the same speed as my peers. My father stifled a laugh. Later that night I found a stack of dusty encyclopedias outside my door, with a sticky note that read *RESEARCH*.

12.

"I don't want you to be the Dungeon Master anymore," Kendall said, standing on the corner where the bus had let us off. He had been building up to something important all afternoon, muttering to himself during the ride home from school. We'd actually avoided talking to each other entirely since the sleepover. We ate our lunches in silence and kicked the tetherball together in a subdued, obligatory way. I wasn't sure either of us knew what the standoff was about, but our silence had gained so much momentum that the sounds of the street faded out as he spoke. The smell of fertilizer and rain on hot concrete drifted on the wind. Kendall's eyes were fixed somewhere just below my chin. His brow was shiny, his round belly stretching and relaxing the fabric of his polo shirt.

"Why not?" I asked, but Kendall stayed quiet. He prodded a caterpillar with the tip of his shoe and wouldn't look at me.

"We can't switch roles," I said. "I'm the one who runs things, and your characters haven't finished my adventure yet."

"Your adventures are stupid," Kendall said, tiny bubbles flecked on his pale lips. "There's never any story—just a bunch of random rooms with stuff in them that make no sense at all."

I groaned. "Kendall, who cares how the goblins got in the room? Who cares what they eat? The point of the game is to kill them and take their treasure, not to write a book report on what they do when you're not around."

"I care," he said, his voice quieter now. "I can't believe in it if it doesn't seem real, if it's all just set up for when we get there."

I'd been relieved that we were talking again, but now that relief vanished. In its place was something like vertigo, deep in my gut, like I was slipping backwards into a dark room without light switches.

"But it *is* all just set up for when we get there," I said. "It's a game we play."

"Well, we suck at it," Kendall said.

A Jeep four-door with its windows down cruised by slowly, then made a U-turn across the median strip a few blocks down. My stomach ached, but my blood was up.

"I want to play with other kids," Kendall said, his eyes on his shoes.

"Fine," I said.

"I mean, with D&D," he said, as if qualifying this took the sting out of his words. "I heard Fat Travis runs a game with some fourth graders."

"Fuck Fat Travis," I said. "And fuck you if you think playing with fourth graders is going to be more fun."

Kendall just stared at his shoelaces. The Jeep made another pass, slower this time, and a shaggy-haired high schooler leaned out the passenger window and shouted *Faggots!* at us.

I took off my backpack, fished out the rest of Casey's stolen printouts, held them up at Kendall like they were tests he'd failed.

"You see this?" I said with real venom in my voice, "You think this isn't just set up for when you see it? You think 'Angela' is real? You didn't have any problem imagining *her* when you were touching yourself the other night."

Kendall made a weird noise, like a cough and a hiccup all at once. I knew I'd said too much, but I could still see the Jeep's taillights in the distance and my skin felt like it was on fire.

"I'm sorry," I said, my voice tired. "I heard you is all."

"I heard you too," he said.

"What are you talking about?"

"You talk in your sleep." Kendall's hands hung loosely at his sides. "You were talking to Casey. You kept saying his name."

I stared at him, then felt my vision go black. I punched the papers into his chest, hard, so he fell backwards onto the pavement with a smacking sound. He gasped in little breaths and stayed there, the pile of printouts unfurling into the grass. He stayed until I left him, and when I turned at the end of the block to look, he was still there, sitting, head bowed, a cloud of naked women dancing like butterflies around him in the afternoon breeze.

13.

Mr. Alphonse was waiting for me at my locker that Friday. I didn't have to ask why, because the evidence had been laid out in a pile of nude printouts, some jammed into the vents of the locker and others in a heap on the hallway floor. A crowd of kids hovered in the doorway of our homeroom, chattering. I remember the weight of Mr. Alphonse's hand on my shoulder as it steered me towards Father Richardson's office, and I remember the way kids' eyes shifted away from mine when I scanned the crowd. I didn't see Kendall, and I couldn't find Casey. By the time we'd left the middle school wing I was shaking, and when the office door opened to reveal Father Richardson's silhouette framed in shadow behind his desk, I began to cry.

My official punishment was detention and a lifelong ban from the computer lab. My parents also grounded me, but since the fight with Kendall I spent most of my time in my room anyway. Teachers spoke to me with a different cadence, with the impatient declaratives they used on the problem students. Ms. Hester still smiled when I asked to use the hall pass, but I imagined that she knew the whole story, and in her knowing there seemed now an unbridgeable distance between myself and that smile.

There was no hero's fate for me as there had been for Fat Travis, either. The consensus amongst my classmates was that I'd stolen the pictures to try and seem cool by taking credit for what Casey had done. For a while, kids would call me names, sometimes try and fight me at recess, but once I started punching back they mostly just let me be. Over time, I learned how to keep my eyes on the middle distance in a crowd. I learned the secret to enduring my own company, and to build around it an envelope of silence that I have carried for a long time since.

14.

I saw Ms. Hester in the paper this morning. I didn't see her so much as I read her name, listed in the Obituaries as the widow of a balding guy named Williams who owned a Ford dealership out in La Place. There wasn't a picture, but I knew it was her. *Survived by his wife, Angela Hester Williams, 49, and their two teenage daughters*, with a condolences address listed below. I read and re-read the obituary, then made tea and called out sick from work. The afternoon passed slowly, and I sat in my kitchen with a pad of my boyfriend's good stationary, doodling as I waited for the words to come. When the sun had set through the boughs of the grapefruit tree, I looked down at what I had done so far: *Dear Angela*, and then, sprouting from the letters, an inky maze of passages and tunnels, pit traps and secret doors, treasure rooms and sleeping monsters that guarded them. Eventually, I heard my boyfriend's keys in the front door. I tore the sheet of stationary and crumpled it into my pocket, putting my bathrobe on and shuffling to meet him with tea in hand and a whisper, *I'm sick, don't get too close, welcome home.*

15.

Casey only spoke to me once more. It was at our 8th grade graduation, during our final alphabetical muster, all of us in chapel and cloaked in the stifling May heat. A rector from our neighboring parish droned on and on, until the sound of pants shifting in church pews became a steady static hiss in the background. I was lost in something feverish. It was a kind of daydream, an accounting of all my former fantasies during the countless gatherings we'd had in these pews, each of them now a strange and anxious shadow cast by shapes I no longer recognized. When the rector finished, Father Richardson stepped forward to applaud the graduating class. A colossal hum filled the room, and Casey turned to me suddenly, his gray eyes alive with light, and said, *finally*.

Hero's Theater

On his break, still in his Spiderman suit, Stackhouse would smoke by the newspaper stand in a shifting parallelogram of shade. To quit smoking altogether took a kind of resolve that Stackhouse didn't feel he had, so he decided instead on those staccato, sideways steps of the insincere quitter. He bought singles at the gas station with his morning Ho Hos. He bummed from guys in suits who stalked the bus stop, checking their watches. He chose lights when he couldn't resist the urge to buy his own, sometimes menthol lights or slims in a fit of social masochism, as if this were a way of embarrassing himself out of the habit. But nothing would deter him. There was something joyous in the punishment of it. He relished the feeling of the smoke in his body, the bitter heat of it in his mouth. At the end of his breaks his lungs would be cinders, his voice a rattle, his step buoyed in dizzy low-gravity as he returned to work, rounding the corner to the back entrance of Celebration Station, into the air-conditioned cavern of joyful, terrible noise.

*

It was a Friday in early September when Stackhouse got called up to the office. Celebration Station had been suffering a slow decline, and non-essential staff were being laid off. It was by some hidden stroke of good fortune that his manager, Ronaldo, had thus far saved his job. Ronaldo wore dress shirts with sleeves that rode up the wrists of his unnaturally long arms. His mustache shone waxy in the thin light of the office that overlooked a labyrinth of arcade games. He'd inherited the job from an uncle who'd come up through corporate, long before Celebration Station expanded to the fast-track suburbs of southern California. It had been Ronaldo's idea to add mini-golf courses, landscaped with imported flora and encircled by blue-dyed lagoons. Ronaldo always spoke to customers with careful words, enunciating in a way that made Stackhouse think he was embarrassed to be from Jalisco. It seemed an obsessive performance of manners. He was fastidious in his ill-fitting shirts, and he never spoke Spanish, even to the families who spoke it to him in confidential tones with wiggling toddlers in tow.

So when Ronaldo called Stackhouse into his office that Friday, Stackhouse had assumed the worst. Several of the temp workers who staffed the superhero performances were already gone, and all the summer-job kids had been cut loose. The interior of the building had taken on the feel of an abandoned casino, beeps and boops echoing between empty corridors of ski ball and skill cranes, the geometric carpeting unblemished by popcorn dust and spilled soda. On the walk up the stairs to Ronaldo's office, Stackhouse was already weighing his options for what to do next, his hands fidgeting with a lighter in his pocket.

"Al, I'm sending you to Long Beach," Ronaldo said when Stackhouse walked in. Nobody called him Al, but this was part of his manager's strange sense of decorum. His employees were all called by first names, which he memorized using a list pinned to the wall to the right of his desk. Several faces and names had a black sharpie X crossed through them.

"Do we have a franchise in Long Beach?" Stackhouse asked.

"No, but it's that or let you go," Ronaldo said matter-of-factly. *Level up and choose your WEAPON* said a voice from the arcade cabinets. Stackhouse shut the door behind him and waited for Ronaldo to continue.

"My cousin is in the party-supply business," Ronaldo said, adjusting in his office chair. "They're expanding, and they want to contract with actors to do the kids' parties. They've already got a couple animal guys on the roll."

"Animal guys," said Stackhouse.

"Nature guys. Brown shirts with all the pockets. Wombats that do tricks, little lambs like pillows. That kind of thing."

"I don't really know any tricks," Stackhouse said. He'd been doing the same thing in his role as Spiderman for a couple of years—a strictly choreographed series of fights on the dinner-theater stage in the party wing of Celebration Station. He had to keep in shape to make the moves look plausible, but all the dialogue was dubbed over loudspeaker so he wasn't too winded to deliver lines with the appropriate gusto. The lines were like cues, numbers in a long dance he performed daily and four times a weekend. *TAKE THAT, GREEN GOBLIN*, kick, step, thrust. *HE'LL BE BACK*, hands on hips, chest out, head nod on the "he" then a look up and to the left.

"You can kick and punch," Ronaldo said.

"I do the script," Stackhouse said. He watched Ronaldo consider him, the mustache rolling a little in each direction as his jaw worked. Beneath his hand were sketches of miniature golf obstacles on cocktail napkins. Ronaldo fidgeted with the napkins, and then reached into his desk, handing Stackhouse a sheet of paper.

"Here's the address," he said. "The party is Sunday, twin boys turning eight. The mom thinks the dad will make a good villain, a bank robber or something. All you gotta do is show up, make some muscles, stop the villain from stealing the presents, bingo, don't do drugs, stay in school, and then drive off."

Stackhouse looked at the address and the details on the paper. Fucking Long Beach.

"It's 100 bucks for a half-hour," Ronaldo said. "More work like it if you do well."

"Gas covered?" Stackhouse asked.

"Just practice some karate," Ronaldo said. "And don't be late."

*

Stackhouse swung by the bank on the way home from Celebration Station that afternoon. There was a Bank of America on almost every corner in his stretch of L.A., but he drove all the way to Century City, another hour in the grinding slog of afternoon traffic, to the branch on Pico. There was a teller he liked to admire from a distance. He'd met her only once, several months ago, when he was out on the west side trying to find a Coin Star machine to convert all the loose change he'd collected from his cup holders. She'd told him the Coin Star service was for BOA account holders only, eyeing the Ziploc in his hand, fat with pennies and sticky with the residue of old soda. Undeterred, he'd opened an account that afternoon, leaving the bank with a smile and $13.52 in a low-interest starter checking account.

She was there when Stackhouse walked in. The bank was packed. It was payday and closing time, and long lines of sweating Los Angelenos shuffled impatiently, doodling on smartphones. Sunlight cut in thin ribbons between the tinted shading on the windows, and after adjusting his eyes, Stackhouse chose a line to the left of his lady teller and settled in for a wait. This suited him fine. Ever since the Coin Star incident, he'd carried a sense of shame about how she'd encountered him. His meager paycheck, emblazoned with his company's name and logo in a cartoon font, seemed childish, a reaffirmation of the first impression he'd given when he carried that Ziploc of loose change up to her. Sun-bronzed, sweaty T-shirt, his graying blond hair swept into an unkempt ponytail—he certainly hadn't cut an impressive figure. Today, he'd made sure he'd brought a sport coat and worn it.

From where he stood, she was almost invisible behind a wide pane of bulletproof glass. She wore horn-rimmed glasses and a tight bun of black hair pressed in a coil to the back of her head. Her skin was pale, and her diminutive body disappeared into an oversized jacket with angular shoulder pads jutting strangely to each side. She was not traditionally pretty, but this appealed to Stackhouse all the more. There was something undiscovered about her, a place for him to imagine her unbuttoned and blossoming as she left the bank. She would be haloed in the chemical pink L.A. sunset, her ridiculous jacket under one arm, striding across the blacktop and away, and to where? To drinks and dancing with her other teller friends? To Malibu Canyon for night surfing? To a quiet apartment overlooking the valley, for dinner with cats and late night internet romance?

Of all the fantasies he'd had about her, the recurring one involved him wearing the Spider Man suit under his dress clothes to the bank. He'd stand in her line, make casual conversation with other patrons, smile and let the red neckline peek through the unbuttoned top of his work shirt. He'd roll his outer sleeve up when he endorsed his check, following her eyes to the sleeve of his spider suit. She'd suck her teeth, trying to look unimpressed, counting cash into an envelope, licking her thumb in slow motion to separate the bills. Sometimes he imagined saying "keep 'twenty for yourself," which seemed risky but the kind of thing a vigilante crime-fighter might say. He liked the conspiracy of it. Maybe she would keep more than twenty for herself. Maybe she was hatching a scheme to make off with some seed money of her own. Bank of America certainly could afford to lose it. There were more BOAs than there were Jack in the Boxes in Los Angeles, more shiny ties and humming lobbies than carwashes.

Inevitably, at the end of his fantasy, she would hand him his cash with only the slightest of smiles—one meant to be interpreted more than seen, just a tick of that pearl skin around her lips. But she'd let her fingers graze his, feel the webbed latex of his sleeve, the secret beneath the dress shirt. And he'd turn away, imagining her eyes on him even as her voice carried over the crowd, *next in line please, welcome to Bank of America, my name is Patricia, how can I help you?*

*

"Mister, I can't practice if you're going to sit there and listen."

Stackhouse blinked. The little girl who'd been sitting on the porch was now standing by his car window, holding a clarinet in one hand. She was pudgy, rounded in the middle, with flushed cheeks and golden hair that was bobbed in the back. She smacked her lips a little when she spoke, and the mouthpiece of the clarinet glistened in a way that turned Stackhouse's stomach. He put away the folding map he'd had in his lap and pointed past her at the house.

"Your mom and dad home?"

She stared at him but said nothing, her eyes half-lidded.

"Do you have twin brothers? Tommy and Kalen? Is it their birthday tomorrow?"

She stared at him harder for a moment. He tried smiling, but felt the acne-scarred skin on his cheeks resist the effort. He tasted his bad breath, and felt hot all over.

"Who are you?" the girl asked, head titled down, one foot drifting uncertainly back towards her porch. Stackhouse noticed strange marks on her wrists—faded purple bruises in the shape of a hand. Her fingers tapped the clarinet nervously.

"Please just get your folks if they're home," Stackhouse said. "I'm part of the birthday party."

She gave him a supremely skeptical look, but trudged back up the steps to the porch, weaving her way past stacks of cardboard boxes overflowing with lawn ornaments and old sneakers. After a minute, a thin man in a polo and jean shorts came out. He was balding but young, with a rim of black hair around the sides of his head and his eyes hidden by dark aviator glasses. He strode purposefully to the car and leaned down to the window, his hands pushing the door shut just as Stackhouse was about to get out. Behind his glasses, his eyes appraised the interior of Stackhouse's car.

"Why are you parked in front of my house and why are you talking to my daughter?" the man said.

"I'm Al Stackhouse, I work for Celebration Station," Stackhouse said, extending his hand awkwardly through the window. "I'm scheduled to work a birthday party at your address tomorrow. I just wanted to swing by and see if you had any special requests or instructions."

"You're Spiderman?" the man asked, his eyebrows arched behind his glasses.

"I'm Al Stackhouse," Stackhouse said, "but yeah I play Spiderman in the Theater of Heroes at Celebration Station."

The man chewed his lip for a moment then stepped back from the window, inviting Stackhouse out of the car. He smiled and shook his hand, his posture now relaxed and jaunty, his legs bowed a little at the knees.

"I'm Chip," the man said. "My youngest boys have their big eighth tomorrow. We want to make it a good show. You know any moves?"

"Moves?"

"Karate and shit."

"We do choreographed fights at the Theater of Heroes, so yeah I spose I do."

"Show me one."

"A move?"

"Yeah."

"Here?"

"Yup. Just a quick one."

Stackhouse eyed him, then glanced around the block. It was a hot Saturday afternoon, and there were kids running in a sprinkler down the street in the half-shade of a desiccated palm tree.

"Come on, you won't hurt me," Chip said. He flexed his arms, sinewed cords popping out against his skin. He was still smiling. Behind him up on the porch, the girl with the clarinet had reappeared in the doorway. Stackhouse shrugged and then stepped back to the edge of the curb, dropping into a ready stance and moving his hands in front of his face, as if he were swatting flies in slow motion.

He thrust one hand out and then another, quick jabs with a knifehand, then a palm strike at an imaginary attacker from behind. As he moved, his eyes drifted back to the little girl, her pudgy skin grayed out in the shade, her face inscrutable, those marks on her wrists like bracelets.

"*Hwaaaaaaa*" Chip said, his glasses flashing in the sun.

*

The Saturday night ritual of VFW poker was cancelled. Otis and Reggie and several of the other veterans had come down with a stomach flu that was going around the nursing home and the game was a no-go. Stackhouse was relieved, and yet he felt a twinge of apprehension. Though he'd needed to prepare for the birthday party, he'd dragged his heels on calling Otis about the poker game. He liked the poker game. They'd had a re-buy tournament running for several weeks and he was 2nd to high-man. But it wasn't necessarily missing the chance to win money that suddenly bothered him. Nor was it camaraderie exactly, though he appreciated the chain smoking and the dirge-like re-telling of war stories.

Perhaps what bothered him now was the commitment this newfound free time suddenly thrust upon him. *Practice some karate*, Ronaldo had said. *More work like it if you do well.* He pictured himself in Ronaldo's office, walking through the steps of a kata. He pictured Ronaldo's unimpressed mustache, his napkin scribbling. In the half-light of his efficiency apartment, Stackhouse felt the whole situation was fishy somehow. There were doubts everywhere that he couldn't seem to pin down, and a strange discomfort about the house he'd visited that day. Why him and not someone younger? Maybe that teenage kid who played a henchman of Dr. Octopus? He was definitely in better shape. Was Ronaldo really giving him a chance for a new job? Was he setting him up to fail?

He drank the remaining beers in his fridge, practicing his balance with a can on his palm while he stepped through his progressions. Then he put the beers down and did some tumbles. After a few rolls he was dizzy, and he found himself standing unsteadily at the window, watching his belly heave while the lights of the freeway crawled beyond in the darkness. There was a churning in his gut, and a strange, hot feeling in his lungs. He recognized that he was at least a little drunk because it occurred to him that maybe he hated the pale figure reflected in his window. He felt old, yet he looked nothing like his own father. No high and tight, a jawline less grim than reluctant. His father had kept his military shape until his seventies and lived in a Spartan apartment down in Montecito that had a chin-up bar in the kitchen doorway. Stackhouse knew his father only as a shadow, as words that weren't spoken, a hard case that died stoically on his couch from an embolism. Yet he was a man whose former life in the Marine Corps occupied the minds of those who met him. His rigid silence and empty apartment begged to Stackhouse; the skin of his knuckles was ridged with violence that Stackhouse could only dream about. Stackhouse blinked at his wavering reflection. Would any child picture him thwarting a bank robbery, really? Would any woman take him night surfing at Malibu Canyon? Would anyone touch his pinpricked face in the water, whisper a salt kiss into his ear, watch the neon moon glitter on the black waves that pulled them out to sea?

Before he knew it, Stackhouse was slipping into his sweatpants and tennis shoes. He grabbed his keys. He swung his arms like windmills as he took the steps, two at a time, down to the front yard. There, the night settled onto him. The dull hum of airplanes lining up at LAX echoed across the valley, the pulse of tires on the highway beating in clip clop time. Sprinklers whirred. He breathed deeply, tasted Los Angeles, stepped onto the road, and started running.

*

The plan was less simple than Chip had originally suggested. A whole backyard production had been cobbled together since Stackhouse stopped by yesterday, and now an elder sibling of the birthday boys was going to play Peter Parker. The kid wore black-rimmed glasses and a pocket-protector, gangly-limbed like his father, but excited for the role. The wife—a redheaded woman who wore long sleeves despite the heat—played the teller of a bank where the birthday presents were kept. Gangly Peter Parker was supposed to sneak around the alley and observe Chip, dressed in a black ski mask and carrying a sackcloth with a dollar sign on the side as he pilfered the presents. The wife would shriek and swoon, and Peter Parker would make a show of taking a few photographs before ducking through the sliding glass doors into the house. There he was supposed to trade places with Stackhouse, who was to tumble out the open door into the yard, shout some ad-libbed lines, and earn his money.

There were a lot of kids at the party. Loud music played from a stereo by a chocolate cake that wilted in the heat. The AC was on high in the house, and a voice shrieked *DOOR CLOSED PLEASE* each time the patter of bare feet entered the kitchen. Stackhouse had been given the parents' room to change and await his cue. He'd arrived fifteen minutes early with his spider suit already on beneath a windbreaker and jeans. Now in full costume, he paced the floor of the tiny bedroom, his toes working the shag fabric of the carpet. He kept checking himself in the mirror, practicing made-up yoga moves, yet he found himself more nervous than he'd ever been for a performance at Celebration Station. He kept pulling his mask up to breathe, his grizzled lips wet with perspiration despite the chilly air that settled from the vent above him.

He eyed the top drawer of the dresser. Women's underwear. A package of cigarettes. His heart pounded. He let his fingers rest on the wood, let one touch the plastic edge of the cigarettes, another rest against the soft lace. He smelled dryer sheets.

"Oh no, we're being robbed!" came a woman's voice from the back yard.

Stackhouse felt a hot rush on his skin, but his hands lingered in the drawer.

"Quiet, you!" came Chip's voice, "I've cut the alarm so there's no one coming to the rescue!"

Stackhouse felt suspended for a moment, his lungs burning for air, smoldering now as his eyes drew level with the mirror one more time. He could see his belly moving in the suit, sagging in and out like a red and blue water balloon. He felt his knees begin to wobble, imagined suddenly just leaving, sneaking out the front door while everyone was distracted. If he was going to run it was going to have to be now. Fuck Ronaldo. But it would have to be now. Right now. As he lifted his hand from the drawer it brushed against a piece of paper taped to the dresser. It was a crayon drawing, a girl in a blue triangle of a dress, a smiley face with short yellow hair, reaching up. Next to the girl, a black stick figure of a man stood, reaching down, its fingers like sideways parentheses, holding her hand. The man figure was gigantic, and the strokes of his black hand swallowed the end of her outstretched arm. Stackhouse stared at the picture.

Suddenly, there were footsteps. Then the door swung open and a breathless Peter Parker, all knees and elbows, came stumbling in.

"Ok, man," he gasped, as if he'd run a mile before reaching the room, "you're up!"

Stackhouse felt his knuckles pop, and he moved his lips but all that escaped was a hiss. The kid looked at him, an odd expression on his face. Then Stackhouse pulled his mask down, pushed into the hall, took a running start, and leapt for the opening in the sliding door.

He felt the wind and then the ground. Someone screamed. For a moment he was paralyzed as he came out of his roll. Then he heard cheering, and he swung his head around, peering through the black screen eyes of his mask at a bobbing mass of happy white faces. They clapped and hooted. He swung his head to the left, where adults stood off by the fence, beers in hand, watching him approvingly. He swung his head back, theatrically this time, like a snake, towards the house, and the cheering continued. He flexed. He spun his hands like blades and the whirled onto the lawn, where Chip crouched by the sack of presents. Chip seemed unsure of where this was going, so he just hovered, and Stackhouse felt his body moving without the need to tell it what to do, circling Chip in a half-crouch, crab-walking until he blocked the exit to the alley.

Get him Spider Man!

Don't let him take my presents!

Kick his ass, guy!

Damon, shut UP.

Chip had stopped with his back to the house now, following Stackhouse's lead, holding the sack over his shoulder like a dark, spindly Santa Claus. He nodded slightly. Stackhouse felt the finale approaching and advanced. As he did, his eyes moved to an upstairs window overlooking the yard. There was a face in the window. A pale moon of flesh. Golden hair, flat gray eyes. Her nose was pressed against the glass, her chin resting on purpled wrists as she watched him. For an instant the world went silent, and Stackhouse felt something pull loose in his guts. His lungs seemed to catch fire. The girl's eyes watched him take hold of Chip's shoulder. They watched, unblinking, as his fist balled up tight, then fell like a hammer against Chip's jaw. He looked up at her eyes again. Still there. They watched the empty moments between swings, as his arms now rose and fell, the impact of each blow shuddering through his whole frame. They watched him push Chip against the edge of the porch with his foot and then land a haymaker that sent a spindle of blood across the sunbaked wood. Though Stackhouse's eyes were now closed, though he mouthed silent syllables he did not understand, he knew they were still there, watching him. He knew, long past the sudden weight of arms around his body, past the taste of grass clippings and the scorched breath of his wordless howl, past the darkness that followed.

Missed Connections

For Other Options, Press Star

Listen: I'm not going to come see you in jail whenever the cops finally catch up to you, so here's how it is. You fucked me, Al. I've been left by two wives, and neither of them fucked me like this. Lupe slept with the guy who delivers those plastic balls for the Kidzone ball pit on my office desk, and you know what? I got a new desk. Lupe was all appetite. I think you met her at the employee cookout—she wasn't the biggest lady there, but I knew exactly what I was getting with her. She told me once she needed three of me in order to be happy. One to make love to her twice a day, one to fix the roof that the goddamned shady inspector ignored, and one to *bring home the bacon*, which for me means 50 hours a week in this bullshit carnival of screaming toddlers and broken skill cranes. I cannot be three men, Al, but this is a known fact for me. So when Lupe fucked that ball-delivery guy, it hurt, but it didn't break me. I'm a firm believer that the world tells you what it is if you listen, and Al, I am good listener.

Did you think that saving you during layoff bingo was easy? Did you know that even after all the temp workers, I still had to let go of ten employees just to get us into the next year? Your name was there, Al. Along with Javier and Raul and a whole bunch of guys who probably thought they were safe because their manager wasn't a heartless fucking gringo who vacationed with a rifle at the border. Thankfully, I feel like only half an asshole because it was a business decision—Javier is too fat, and Raul couldn't remember the Spiderman routine if we bought him a tutor, so it was stick with you or cancel our contracts for the birthday parties. I spent a week looking at your file, your 10 years acting with the company, your goddamn photograph on my wall, and thought ok, he's a grown man, he's steady, he knows what he is. I wish I'd flipped a fucking coin.

You know, when I first hired you, I did it because you didn't look like a superhero at all. I mean, you were in OK shape, but I'd have pictured you more as a longshoreman, or a grocery clerk, or one of those banditos that work the exhaust-inspection stations and make you get shit fixed at their brother's garage before they'll pass you. Maybe I was in a weird place then, but I had this little voice in my head that I couldn't shake. It sounds like corny shit us ugly people tell ourselves, but every superhero-looking prettyboy I ever knew beat his wife or sold used cars or something. Every last one of them sat around waiting for things to be handed to them. Guys like you could be used car salesmen too, but I could tell just by looking that you didn't have much handed to you. You told me once that your father served, and I knew what that meant. Mi abuelo landed at Guadalcanal and Tarawa, the only mexicano in his platoon; lost two fingers but still made sure my papa knew enough to fear laziness and ingratitude. So I looked at you, all those acne scars, the way you took your cigarette breaks alone, and thought—why not him?

Anyway, the family's bringing a civil suit. Family lawyers came after me too, but technically you were working a contract job off-the-books for my cousin, so I think I dodge d that bullet. The hardest part is my cousin thinks I'm worthless now, que yo no sirvo para nada, and that's on you, Al. I vouched for you, and now he's got some guy's wife calling him every day in tears. You broke that guy's whole face, did you know that? His whole face, not just his teeth or his jaw, but his cheeks, those bones around his eye socket. I never imagined in a million years that you had it in you. But I suppose you'll need it wherever you're hiding out now. There are probably more faces to break before it's done.

I should also tell you, I went by your place yesterday. The landlord had all your stuff out on the curb and a For Rent sign up already, got into me quick about money you owed. He was pissed, kept talking slow to me like I didn't speak English. Real politician, that guy. I gave him 20 bucks and took your stuff away—not the consignment couch or the chairs, just the boxes. Still not sure why I did that for just for some jeans and a few boxes I won't open. Shit is just sitting there, waiting in my garage. I'm not going to tell you where I live, and I'm not going to tell you where in the side garden my kids leave the spare house key. I will tell you that I have a carry permit, and that I once beat a gangbanger with a garden hose till he puked when he tried to steal my lawnmower. Maybe I'll never see you again. Maybe you're gone for good, and maybe that's good fucking riddance.

Maybe your boxes will be gone one day when I come home—usually by 6:00 on weekdays, the kids with their grandmother till 4:30, and all day on Sundays.

City of Long Beach Police Department

Daily Activity Log:__Sunday__9/13/13__
4:34:00 PM
Dispatch #: 10982
Subj: ANIMAL CALL /GENERAL DISTURBANCE
Disposition: Unable to locate
Location Address: 1460 Marietta Ct., Long Beach, CA
Location Apartment #: NA
Details:

CALLER's dog escaped, worried that animal control will euthanize it. CALLER was advised to query animal control directly; CALLER became uncooperative, used expletives at dispatch. CALLER also claimed a man in a Halloween costume broke his fence and let the dog out, claimed an altercation between neighbors kept him from retrieving the dog. Dispatch notified a possible 217 with injuries at neighboring address. Officers on scene reported no sign of a man in a Halloween costume, or of the dog.

TO: Tall and Handsome From the Birthday Party Fight

I saw you at the backyard party, the one where Chip Hostetler got his jaw broke by that maniac in the Spider-Man suit. You were kind enough to stick around and help clean up, which probably meant more to Angela than she had time to tell you, what with her husband in the ambulance and the cops taking statements from everyone one-at-a-time right there on the lawn so the whole neighborhood could see. I think I was hiding behind the poplar tree. I know I was crying, but most of the parents got pretty emotional that afternoon so maybe that doesn't narrow it down. I was wearing a black cotton top and those silly banana croc sandals. Angela's little girl picked them out for me when we went shopping at the ped mall in Santa Monica last spring. I wore them for her, but she ended up spending the party in her room anyway. I suppose that was for the best.

Anyhow, what made me think of you was your hands. Not in a creepy way, I promise, I don't normally go to kids' birthday parties and watch the hands of good-looking men. I mean, I noticed you certainly—you're young for having a child the same age as the Hostetler twins, and I have a weakness for tall men who are thin the way you are. If I may say so, you look naturally strong, the way men in old photos looked before all the weight rooms and wax jobs. You wear your clothes the right way, and I could tell by the veins on your wrists that you're all wires. Women notice these things, believe me, and it says a lot about you that you aren't dressing to flaunt it either. But really, I suppose what I mean about your hands was the way they moved with confidence—the way they went to work once the police were gone and the families left and there was just the yard covered in cake plates and the gaggle of us who stayed to comfort Angela. I didn't see if you were one of the men who piled on Spider-Man, but I saw you helping out afterwards, saw the way you spoke calmly, the way you took on one task and then another. I even watched you try to scrub the blood off the deck. I know you did your best.

Back when I was still with Eugene, we went to visit his father at the hospital during the chemo. He was a hard case, Eugene's dad. You got the sense he'd fought things his whole life just for the sake of fighting, and cancer was no different. Anyway, one of our visits Eugene's dad had some kind of seizure in the middle of a meal, rolled right onto the TV remote and maxed it out until all we could hear was audience applause. He thrashed hard enough to pull free of his tubes, and all the alarms went off. There was some orderly, some nurse's aid, who Eugene Sr. managed to vomit all over when they tried to clear his airway. We were horrified, of course, but Eugene thought the old man was doing it on purpose, just shouted at him to stop putting on such a show while he searched for the plug to the television set.

It's the orderly whom you reminded me of, that day at the Hostetler's party.

I suppose it could've been that you were trying to scrub blood out of a splintery deck, but I don't think that's it. I think it was before, when you ushered Angela inside, when you started cleaning up without asking anyone about it, the way you moved around the police and the shrieking kids and the general chaos like they were pieces in a still life. Like that orderly, who I could see had some flecks of vomit on his cheeks and lips, but who held the old man's shoulders while the doctors shouted, while Eugene cursed at the TV set, while the old man thrashed and foamed and we all thought we were going to have to watch the Lord snatch a life away right there in front of us.

After they stabilized Eugene Sr. and wheeled him out, a woman a few rooms down on the ward had a birthday party. Eugene was pretty upset, slammed the door when the singing started, but I found a real comfort in hearing it. We listened to them sing while the orderly mopped the floors and changed the old man's bed sheets. The music was like the traffic out the window, that 101 overpass that's always crawling even at 11:00 in the morning; there was this world, going about its business. Not immune to our horrible scene, or ignoring it, but a part of it, like the hands that carefully stacked chocolate cake plates and wiped themselves on the leaves of the poplar tree, where I stood like a statue in the shade, the heavy heat of the sun spinning off our shoulders and holding us together, just for a moment.

Error code<40911353> Delivery Failure Notification

This is an automatically generated delivery status notification:
Delivery to the following recipients failed:

Pkellybelly@hotmail.com

Technical details: see error code ref

--------------------------------Original Messge------------------------------

From:

Ethel M. Baumann
West Coast Regional Manager, Southern District
Human Resources
Bank of America
100 N. Tryon St.
Charlotte, NC 28202

To:

Ms. Patricia Keller

Teller, Junior Loan and Sales Associate

Century City Branch
2049 Century Park E
Los Angeles, CA 90067

Sub: Termination of Services

Dear Ms. Keller,

Our previous letter, attached below, may be referred to with regards to management having advised you of unsatisfactory practices in customer relations, citing several specific instances in which account holders voiced complaints about lapses in professionalism and "unnecessarily brusque and/or impolite" encounters. HR was notified that your manager has spoken with you, and we're sure you are aware of company policy regarding the decorum and personability of our associates. Since your manager has reported "no positive improvement" in the situation, we regret to inform you that your services have been terminated with immediate effect. You may obtain clearance forms, severance, and information about COBRA health options from your local HR representative.

Our bank is a family, and the treatment of our customers is an extension of our family values. While we recognize the extenuating circumstances brought to our attention concerning your mother's ongoing treatment, we cannot abide a member of our family's failure to adhere to the core principles of respect and courtesy. On a personal note, I'd like to add that I have also had a loved one battle with Alzheimer's, and understand the ways this can try one's faith beyond what we might think possible to endure. I suggest you reflect upon Romans 12:12, *Be joyful in hope, patient in affliction, faithful in prayer*, and in time, you may come to know the wisdom of Revelations 3:10, *Since you have kept my command to endure patiently, I will also keep you from the hour that is to come upon the whole world to test those who live upon the earth.* I have also attached a link to in-patient facilities at White Springs Alzheimer's Center, with Dr. Mankevicz's email and contact information—he is a family friend, and would be happy to give you a breakdown of their services, amenities, and payment plans.

Wishing you the best in your future endeavors,

Ethel M. Baumann

Email sent: 9/17/13 5:05PM   Attachments (2)

---------------------------------End Original Messge------------------------------

The Napkin Note

I know your name is Patricia, that I am welcome in Bank of America, that you want to help me. I want to help you, too. I'm going to re-write this when I'm not drinking, clean up the language and make it more beautiful to read, but for now it's more important just to say these things while I've got them in my head. There's this bartender at the Cozy Inn—the little cop bar with all the Christmas lights on Washington just off Sepulveda—this Asian girl who seems to know everyone.

I tip her two bucks a beer, but most of the regulars don't seem to tip at all, and yet she's still just as friendly as if they did, touching their hands when she serves the beer, doing a hip-shake when she fishes around in the cold case. I used to get mad about this, thought they were ungrateful. But then I started to see it another way, like a family at dinner that stopped saying grace or thank you after someone passed the salt—not because they were rude, but because the whole thing was understood without anyone saying it out loud. Maybe that's the situation at the Cozy Inn too. But then I start feeling like a shithead, Patricia, because here I am giving this woman two bucks extra for MGD bottles and thinking *this means I'm an outsider*. I'm ashamed by being generous, I start to think that when she thanks me she's just putting on an act. Does that make sense? Like, whose lost puppy do I need to find to get into that club, where understandings are made and everyone touches each other and smiles and knows what it all means?

Do people tip you? Do you know what it is that I'm asking you? Everything about your bank feels like this big play. I know a bit about plays, so believe me on this. It's a big, expensive production—everyone gets a hug from their rich Uncle BOA, and we come away rich, as if the suits you wear might grow on our own skin too. But where you work, all the courtesy and confidence doesn't mean we're family; it means we're the tippers. We're on this side of the bulletproof glass, after all. And maybe you are too, because I've seen the car you drive, and nobody drives a Ford Taurus to Uncle BOA's Thanksgiving dinner.

Things are changing. I lost my old job yesterday (no more clown-colored *Funterprises Inc.* checks for you to deposit!), but start a new one tomorrow and it's the kind of thing that can really change a man. I've been acting in a routine so long I can't even remember when it started, and all the steps in that routine have begun to feel like they're parts of me, like extra limbs or warts or something. I bet you know something about routines too, Patricia. But routines are only good for the folks on the right side of the glass, for the cops at the Cozy Inn—not for people like you and me. We are the actors, we are the ones who can say *Fuck you, Ronaldo*, with a smile and a handshake, we are the ones who can round off the decimals and bide our time until Uncle BOA isn't looking. Do you understand what I'm saying? Do you hear it? We are the ones whom the world calls.

–Al

Run Spider-Man Run

By Kalen Hostetler

3rd Grade English, Mrs. Popadopalous

Spider-Man wanted my birthday cake but Mom and Chip said NO CAKE FOR YOU SPIDER-MAN so he got angry. Moms and Dads shouted. My brother Tommy ate two pieces of cake when he was supposed to have one and then he ran away and Spider Man punched Chip and everybody went OOOOOOO and NOOOO. Tommy ate Makayla's cake too. Makayla gets sick a lot and hogs the upstairs bathroom. I never got to have a piece of cake because all the Dads tried to tackle Spider-Man like a football game. But Spider-Man is the best football player, and he pushed Uncle Damon and he fell into the fence and broke the fence and Uncle Damon barfed and Spider-Man ran into the neighbor's yard and their dog Rufus got out and the policemen came and Mom made me go inside.

In conclusion, Spider-Man lives in a tree by Big Bear Lake where Chip takes us camping in summertime. He has a tree house made of webs, and he is there now with lots of cake that he stole.

The End.

June 13th, 1970

Katherine,

I'm giving this letter to a support company guy who went AWOL a few months back, so if this gets to you it means that guy actually earned his 100 bucks. It's weird writing for the first time without the censors. I'm so used to saying just the basics that saying more feels like the lie, if that makes any sense. Not that the basics were really lies either. The basics now are: I am alive. I'm still in-hospital with III Corps, which I suppose means nothing to you, but trust me that it means

I'm off the line and surrounded by a lot of guys who are stupider, fatter, and slower than me. They're my canary in the coal mine, as your mom would say. The good news is that my ankle is healing fine, and I probably won't be forward deployed again anytime soon.

How are you and little Al? The last letter that made it through was in January, posted from your mother's place. Sgt. Fuckstick joked that the censors got to you too, since it barely made a page. Is Al enrolled for Kindergarten yet? Did you put him in that Jewish school? I'm glad Mr. Jefferies shoveled the walk for you and all, though I don't want him thinking we owe him anything. If you still see him, tell him I will pay whatever's fair for the work when I'm back. I won't have Al growing up thinking we rely on the charity of librarians and knitting clubs.

I think of Al at the stupidest times now that I'm laid up without much else to do. When I was in Tay Ninh we could hear the bombs falling over the border to the east every morning since April. Bombs sound different than artillery, they cluster all together, they wiggle your coffee and rattle your chest if you're lying down. We hear the bombs and I think of Al with the sandcastles at Fire Island, stomping around in those ridiculous gumboots. *Boom boom boom* they'd go. I daydream about carrying him on my shoulders in a Huey, about moving his little feet with my hands as the ordnance flashes in the hills. Maybe that's a horrible idea to you. It's hard sometimes to think about the normal things without also thinking about the war, they kind of all happen on top of themselves now. Kids chase a dog in the street here with a machete and I think about the Easter egg hunts at your mother's. I think this will change, though, when I am home.

I'll admit, I started this letter a little angry. Maybe nothing I've written has gotten through to you. Maybe some asshole in Quan Long has a stack of your letters and jerks off to the pictures. I've felt this urgency, especially now, and I can't take all the lying down and sweating out the days. I can feel myself getting fat. You'd be disappointed. But it's Al I think about the most, so maybe you and I are alike in that way. It feels like all the strings on a big sweater are coming loose at the same time, and I need him to know some things about the sweater before it all gets unraveled. We are going to lose the war. That's the first thing. The second is that the only thing anyone can be in this world is a coward or a motherfucker, and most people don't get a choice. Like, they get sucked into it, like they're on the path before their feet are even on the ground. Cowards mean well. Motherfuckers cut you for a cigarette. Cowards get hometown funerals. Motherfuckers carry the coffins.

But you tell him. Al, I mean, you tell him that my eyes are open now. Tell him that there will come a time when he will know what this war was and what it wasn't, and his eyes will be open too, and when that time comes he's going to be something different than whatever passes for men back home. He will be a rare species. He will crush sandcastles. You tell him this.

I will look for you at your mother's when I ship back in November, and if you're not there, I'll know the story even if I never get another letter from you. If you try to take Al with you, know that there is not a place you can go that I will not find him. We have been well-trained here. We are built with the right parts. And because Al is a little piece of me, I believe that he will find me too. It comforts me to know it, and I dream at night of those little feet, of the hard, hard steps.

Al, Off the Grid

The security camera at Morrison's Party Rentals is lonely. Its job is to document its own solitude. Or its job is to enforce its own solitude, and the record of this job becomes a movie that no one watches, hours-long footage of an oblong square of concrete. The star of the movie is the beer can that cartwheels across the sidewalk in a gust of wind, or the frantic shadow of the hornet building its nest in the lee of the drainspout. The tapes get downloaded each morning, stored on an old hard drive collecting dust in the manager's office. Eventually, at the suggestion of a drinking buddy, the manager buys a motion-sensor trigger for the camera, ends up saving hours of empty footage each night. Now the movies become vignettes. The story of double-bagged garbage and a persistent raccoon. The story of Dale Perkins' little brother learning that a Sharpie doesn't keep a straight line on brick façades the way he'd imagined, and the sequel in which he edits the giant penis he's drawn with a can of Rust Oleum so that it looks more like a giant penis. The story of rats, of falling ice, of pigeons startled by lightning storms in summer. The stop-motion details of the seasons creep by in the background, motifs about the patience with which nature plays the long game.

The robbery footage begins with Al crossing the parking lot from the south. He's hooded and dressed in layers, his gym bag tied with a bungee cord across his back like an arrow-quiver. He cuts a tangent across the lot between Parkview Baptist and the Hardee's on 7th, then when the motion sensor trips again he's back, licking a hamburger wrapper and looking at something through the windows of Morrison's. A pair of headlights sweep across the lot and Al bends over to tie a shoelace. Once the darkness settles in again, he stands up straight and looks around. The hamburger wrapper flutters off in the breeze. Then he drops into the posture of a boxer, his knees flexed, his arms extended forward and rotating in little circles in the air. He lifts a knee and sweeps gracefully backward, tiptoeing in a pattern, his hands striking invisible enemies that approach him from each side, his lips moving like he's counting out the steps of a dance. Finally, he leans back and puts his leg through the plate glass window. The camera flips off during the time he's inside the store, then clicks on again as he emerges through the empty window frame with a Spider-Man suit tucked under one arm.

Insurance covers the window. The register and the safe are untouched. Bits of glass wedge into the cracks in the pavement, flickering like stars in the light of the Hardee's sign. Sometimes late at night, when his mind won't let him sleep, the manager gets up and makes himself a drink. He'll sit at his basement table in the dark, turn on his desktop, and watch the footage of the man in front of his store window. The man will do his dance in an endless loop. The manager will feel the bourbon hug his heart, think about the journey that Spider-Man suit is taking. On his way back to sleep, he'll catch himself moving his hands in slow circles, sweeping aside the ghosts in his hallway, swimming himself back to the warmth of his bed.

*

When in public, Al occupies himself with the invented errands of the lonely. Several slow walks downtown to mark the time, with stops at Java Junction on each way for some shade, some spare change, and the sounds and smells from inside that he's come to associate with one another. He'll leave his gym bag in a public locker at the YMCA and wait around in case he has a chance to grab a shower. If it's too busy at the Y, he'll hike out Route 6 to the interstate junction and angle for a shower at the Flying J truck stop. The days are a steady orbit around town, with tangents into alleys every so often to relieve himself. Over the course of the summer, Al shows up in four videos and twenty-six pictures.

In two of these pictures he is in the shade of a massive cottonwood near the border of Oakland Cemetery. He likes to sleep under that tree if he didn't get to sleep the night before. In the first picture he is doing just that, a reclined silhouette on the rise behind a couple from Davenport who have stopped on a drive west to their son's graduation at the Air Force Academy. In the second he's awake, his chin in his hands, watching from an eastward angle as a man in his mid-40's poses a teenage girl with dark lipstick and a leather collar beneath a weathered statue of an angel. The man recruited the girl online, posing as a photographer interested in the erotic and the occult. Unbeknownst to the girl, the man takes an extra picture through the foliage when they're done, with a vague inkling that he's witnessing something else worth seeing: here now a stranger with stringy blonde hair and travel-worn clothes, stooped over where the girl had just been, one hand hovering above the grass where the girl had knelt, one hand on the blackened skin of the angel, gripping the statue's robe until his knuckles shine white.

*

There is security camera footage of him in an Arby's drive-thru, riding in the back of Dale Perkins' black Mustang. Strangely, this footage comes two minutes prior to a daylight robbery in which the cashier is shot in the hand with rock salt when she tries to close the service window on the barrel of a shotgun. The robbers drive a red pickup, idling behind the Mustang in which Al is nothing more than an outline, his head lolling back onto the seat, cradled by a carpet of decaying jeans that have accumulated in the Mustang over the years.

For a little while, police who review the security footage entertain the notion that the black Mustang was a part of the robbery. They note how the driver of the Mustang keeps checking his rearview, and at one point seems to give a thumbs-up out the window towards the pickup. When questioned later, the robbers deny this, saying that one of them had inadvertently struck the horn while loading his shotgun. In a separate interrogation room, the accomplice claims he'd even waved an apology to the car in front of them, and when the interviewing officer laughs at this, the accomplice laughs too, each of them trailing into a cough that tastes of smoke-spit, neither of them entirely unhappy.

*

Because Jahvid has been robbed before, he has a camera in his taxi. He wasn't robbed in his taxi, but his taxi is where he spends most of his time. The camera was a gift from his wife, along with some car-wash coupons and a memory foam cushion for lumbar support. On late nights, with bar-time winding down and the university kids doing their stagger-dance into Clinton Street from the pedestrian mall, Jahvid begins to feel like everything that's ever happened to him has happened to him in his cab. Sometimes he lets this line of thinking wander outward, just to see where it goes. His cab is a spaceship. The lumbar cushion is a storage device for his pain. The surfaces that hold him are haunted. They are like his socks, thick with the residue of idle hours and nervous energy.

It's late summer, early evening, and right now there is a drunk girl in his cab. She is singing, and Jahvid is watching her in the rearview. She forms her words with an underbite, like she's dipping tobacco. Her voice is beautiful. Her eyes are closed, her baby-fat face a silver moon. Jahvid checks to be sure his camera is recording.

Suddenly the dome light of the cab flicks on. Frantic motion in the back, and now a man, lean brown arms and sharp elbows pressing against the cushions of the driver's seat, climbs in next to the girl.

"You've got to follow that car," the man is saying. "There, there, the black hatchback turning out."

Hold me tight, the girl sings, *hug me into your heart*.

Jahvid turns his head, takes in the man's wild mane of hair, his patchwork beard, the drifter's wardrobe of layered shirts and jackets. His scent fills the cab.

"You've got to get the fuck out of my cab," Jahvid says.

The girl opens her eyes, stops singing.

"Not you, honey—" Jahvid starts, but the drifter has pulled out a wad of crumpled bills and is unpeeling them onto his lap. Jahvid guesses forty or fifty bucks in all, guesses panhandling, glances from the money back to the windshield now flecked with rain.

"Please, man," the drifter says, "he's taking her right now."

Outside there's a scuffle between groups of students in front of a bar. A bouncer in a black polo has someone pinned on the pavement, and war-whoops erupt from the gathering crowd. Cellphones come out, pale blue squares bob in the shadows.

Please mannnn, the girl sings.

"The black hatchback," the drifter says again. "It just turned onto Washington. I don't know where he's taking her."

"Buddy, if you need a cop . . . "

Follow that carrrrrrr the girl sings.

"It's everything I've got," the drifter says, taking his money and dropping it onto the seat next to Jahvid. It's closer to one hundred than fifty. The man's eyes are electric in the lights of the dash.

"City limits only," Jahvid says finally, shifting the cab into drive. They round the corner and come to rest several places behind the hatchback. Al fidgets, slumps back into the seat. Cellphone cameras flash on the sidewalk behind them. The girl pats the edge of Al's sleeve affectionately.

"We're going to rescue that girl," she says.

*

The call from the hotel is initially listed as a domestic. Officer Marona is supposed to be dropping a juvenile delinquent back at his home, but he takes the call anyway, leaving the boy in the breakroom with a soda and the Brewers' game on TV. He pulls up to the Rodeway Inn a few minutes later with his lights off. There are two trucks with local plates in the lot, and a shiny black hybrid hatchback that he assumes is a rental. When he steps out of his cruiser, Marona is greeted by the roar of a jetliner, sees the contrail underlit from somewhere far to the west. The sky is a heavy purple, the horizon a gas-station glow. The air is sweet with pesticide. Cicadas hiss and fields of corn ripple in the wind. A pair of raccoon eyes glitter from the alcove behind the dumpster.

"Go away," calls a voice behind 214 after several knocks, "Everybody's fine here."

The manager, who smells of sweat and floral body spray, is fumbling with a key ring next to Officer Marona.

"Come to the door please, sir," the manager says, turning his bald head after speaking to listen for voices inside. After a minute, the bolt pops and the door opens, a girl's head emerging beneath the security chain.

"Like he said . . . Oh shit, Chance, he called the cops."

The girl's mascara is streaked, her cheeks powdered a skeletal white. She wears a leather collar and her hair has been pulled back into a braid, little wisps by her ears spinning in the breeze from the gap in the door. Her eyes take in Marona's posture, the tilt of his head towards his shoulder-mounted radio, the pale reflection of light on the lens of his body camera.

"Ma'am, do you mind if we come in?" Officer Marona asks.

"Everything's fine, Officer," comes the male voice from inside, in a tone that Marona recognizes as not fine at all. "We just had the television too loud."

Marona positions his shoe at the door's edge, relaxes his shoulders, and tries to make eye contact with the girl in the doorway. She's young.

"It is," she says uncertainly, "fine—that is. We're sorry we worried you."

Marona stares at her until her eyes shift to his. Inkwell pupils, the mascara like tiger stripes on the curve of her cheekbones.

"You've been crying?" Marona asks.

"It's hot," she says, pulling her braid tight with the palm of her hand.

"The AC in this room is shit," calls the male voice.

Marona slowly lifts his hand, points to the security chain, nods, pats the air as if he's petting the tension out of the moment. He keeps petting until she sighs, ducks, pushes the door closed and then re-opens it, standing to one side to reveal a disheveled king bed, jewelry and high heeled shoes scattered around the floor, a tripod and an empty camera bag on the table by the window. A thin man, white, maybe in his 40s, pauses from stuffing a backpack with leather lingerie. He's wearing a green short-sleeve polo, khakis, an unbuckled belt. His hairline is thin and combed forward, his forehead shiny. "What the fuck," he says toward the girl, then again toward the room, like he too had just opened the door and found them both this way.

The girl reaches for her purse. "Officer," she says, her voice now shifted to something a little huskier, a little more practiced, "I'm eighteen, here's my license. I'm here because I want to be. Everything really is ok."

Marona flips over the ID in his hands. "You guys having a photoshoot, Miss Wasjeski?"

She glances around the room, ending at the tripod and the table where the camera bag lies turned open, but says nothing.

"Where's the camera?" Marona asks. The girl sighs. The manager retreats to the stairwell, speaking angrily into his cellphone.

"I see liquor bottles on the dresser," Officer Marona says in the clipped, casually-direct cadence of law enforcement, "and one of you has just identified yourself to me as being eighteen."

The AC in the window rattles to life.

"Failure to restrict access to alcohol with a minor present is an arrestable offence," Officer Marona continues, talking past the girl. The man groans and flops backward onto the bed.

"So, does someone want to tell me what's going on, or do we need to take a ride?"

"Officer," the girl says after a pause, her voice almost a whisper, "you're never going to believe us anyway."

*

{tape rolling}

Miss Wasjeski approached me. Online, she found my website. I do *tasteful* erotica, artistic burlesque, other kinds of model-focused photography. I made her no promises.

{inaudible}

Eventually to Salem, Massachusetts. It was a quest we planned together. We share an interest in death and spirituality. I see her gothic self-expression as an act of empowerment, embodying how the feminine mystique frightens ordinary Americans, how it . . .

{inaudible}

Ah, um, all over really. Doom Town, Nevada; Barker Ranch; The Clutter family home in Kansas. We just stopped in Iowa for the Black Angel. That's one of the places she wanted to do a shoot.

{inaudible}

I'd prefer not to discuss that without a lawyer present.

{inaudible}

Divorced. Several years now.

*

Earlier that same afternoon, Officer Marona is dispatched to Southeast for *kids roaming in the street, "looking for something to get into."* When he approaches Mercer Park, his dashboard camera picks up a trail of baloney slices slapped against windshields of parked cars, their skin glowing iridescent in the heat. The trail turns to eggs, then briefly to slices of pizza with some bites taken from them. Marona blurbs his siren when he turns the corner, and ahead of him, shirtless boys in jean-shorts scatter. A chubby kid with overalls stays behind, his hands clutching a now empty grocery bag.

"PopPop gonna be mad about his baloney," the kid says when Marona pulls up. Officer Marona motions for him to get into the cruiser. Then Marona floors it, catching up to one of the shirtless boys in the roundabout of Memory Gardens, the bumper clipping the boy's legs just as he makes it to the cemetery grass. The boy flails as Marona gets to him, his pale goblin-belly flashing in the sun.

"Tell him the eggs was your idea, piggy!" the shirtless boy shrieks as Marona pulls his arms behind his back.

"None of it was my idea," the chubby kid says.

"You said they was rotten!"

The chubby kid's eyes drift up to Officer Marona, then back to his lap. "They was past the date is all."

The shirtless boy swears colorfully for several minutes from the back seat. Marona waits for him to finish, his eyes on the rearview. He knows he doesn't have to try to look angry anymore. All he has to do is just look. At home, or at the house that used to be home, his daughter's 3rd grade family portrait is still taped to the cupboard—a smiling woman, a smiling child, a smiling dog, a smiling sun, and then just a face, a circle with two dots and a line, a mouth as flat as the land, as dead as the heat of August.

"I can make a deal if you let me go," the shirtless boy says, once Marona drops the chubby kid off. "My brother is into all kinds of shady shit."

"We're going to call your folks at the station," Officer Marona says to the rearview.

"Ain't nobody to call."

"You live alone?"

"With my shady-shit brother. Dale Perkins. Y'all know him."

Officer Marona keeps driving.

"But others too," the boy says.

"Oh yeah?"

"Dale picks up the Mexicans down by Home Depot, takes 'em out to wherever they doing work each day."

"They live with you too?"

"Nope. Just some Jesus-looking drifter Dale picked up. Does a karate dance every morning by the window. Pays Dale rent, speaks Mexican to the Mexicans."

"I'm not interested in drifters or Mexicans," Officer Marona says. He makes a noise like a laugh, but it comes out as a sigh, and once it's out he doesn't add anything more. The boy seems to be waiting on him, but Marona's train of thought has suddenly switched tracks, and now he's imagining a different scene, one where he stops at Arby's instead of Iowa City Police headquarters, where he buys Dale Perkins' little brother a milkshake and makes him eat it, where he gets one too, because he's hungry and there's no longer anyone at home now to tell him he can't or shouldn't or that he needs to think about what kind of example he's setting when he comes home with no appetite for casserole. Marona imagines the frozen ache in his temple, the squeak of the chairs, the stories the boy would tell him. In this scene, he believes there is something he could say to the boy. There are words he knows, if he could only think of which ones to pick and how to arrange them, but he can't. He feels this lack like he's always known it, like he hates himself for thinking otherwise. Behind him, a car honks.

"Green light, asshole," says Dale Perkins' little brother.

*

Several weeks earlier, Al's sunburned legs appear in the background of a video chat in Dale Perkins' living room. There isn't much furniture, save for a computer in the corner where Dale Perkins' little brother is sitting, spread-legged with his hand down his pants, pleading with a girl in Hungary to do the same. Behind him there is a high-backed green couch and a shin-level coffee table, a rat's nest of wires that snake back to the television.

Dale Perkins and Al are sitting on that couch. Dale is drinking a beer and talking to Al, and as far as Al can remember, it's the first real conversation he's had with another human being in months. In this calculation, he doesn't count the cops who've moved him off park benches, or the stories he's made up on street corners for change. He doesn't even count the first work crews he did with Dale, where all he did was translate orders into Spanish, affirm or shake his head, say "thank you" when he got his cash at the end of the day. He's actually gotten good at saying nothing. Good enough that saying something worth saying takes time.

Where do you come from? Dale Perkins wants to know.

Al thinks about his answer, but he guesses Dale doesn't care. He's asking because he's drinking, because he doesn't want to listen to his little brother sex-chat in the corner, because there's an hour to kill before it's time to hop back in the Mustang and pick up the day-laborers.

Who were you before you got here?

This is a question Al feels more than hears, a question he has felt before. It's the kind of thing that hums in the air of each new city he comes to. He feels it as an absence of itself, a certainty in the eyes of strangers that he is only these clothes, this beard, this bag, and the black cracked road.

If he were to answer, Al would want to do so in a way that places him alongside our wishes for his good fortune. He'd want words that color him this way. He'd try something about self-discovery, about waking up to the smallness of one's life and leaving it behind. But these words would be fiction, and below them would be darkness. There is a chance that he is not a good man, and that walking away from a divorce, a friendless poker game at the VFW, an outstanding warrant which sits like a landmine in the police computers of Los Angeles County—that these are the salient details of his life. There is also a chance that this constellation reveals a deeper violence, the plot from home movies he's now forgotten. How funny, he thinks, that he now mixes up the recollection with the dream of things. How funny that memory and imagination are verses of the same song.

*

{tape rolling}

I mean, Chance probably thought he was fooling me, but I got out of

California, you know? Even if it ends today, I'm half a country away from Riverside.

{1st Detective, inaudible}

Easy—older guys are always the ones with all the needs. What gets him off is the wanting. When I let him have it, he's all over the place, gibberish and baby talk. He's got this whole other voice he uses . . .

{inaudible, coughing}

Sorry. I just meant that the whole thing is about him, his needs. He doesn't want to fuck me so much as he wants to want to fuck me. That's why all the pictures. And now, some pyscho kidnapper has the camera . . .

{inaudible}

That's what I told the officer who showed up at our hotel—it didn't make any sense to us either. Chance was in the shower, and the way the guy knocked, I thought it was the hotel manager. He seemed real suspicious, the manager. Doesn't get a lot of father-daughter road trips I suppose.

{2nd Detective, inaudible}

Sometimes, yea, but literally nobody asks. Anyway, when I open the door it's not the manager, but some beardy motherfucker with a gym bag. He's got a Spider-Man suit on, all except the mask, and he starts pushing his way into the room whisper-shouting at me and trying to grab my arms.

{inaudible}

Fuck yes, I screamed. This guy is talking about helping me escape, about taking me back to my mom and dad, which is insane because my mom has been dead since I was thirteen and my dad is conning a bitchy cosmetics executive out of her fortune in Vancouver.

{inaudible}

Where would I recognize him from, a gas station? Our dinner downtown? He was probably some pervert who saw us pull up at an empty motel. I told Chance no more roadside shitholes, but every time that comes up it's all about his money problems and then I just want to stick a pencil in my ear . . .

{inaudible}

Maybe six-one, super thin, blue eyes. Odd, though. He lets me see his face, like he wants me to see it. When Chance comes out to see what's up, the guy pulls his mask down. What do you think that's about?

{inaudible}

Well, I didn't. I got him with pepper spray while he was distracted with Chance—not that Chance was going to do anything physical—even welterweight Spider-Man could probably kick Chance's ass. But the spray drives him crazy, and he's shouting *why why why* and I keep spraying until he grabs the camera off the table and runs.

{inaudible}

Chance wanted to. It was his camera. But that guy was over the fence and gone before either of us knew what to do.

{inaudible}

I don't know yet. Things happen for a reason, you know? You gotta look out for signs, read what the world is telling you. It's been an adventure. I'm still going to see Salem, assuming you're not arresting me . . .

{2nd Detective, inaudible}

That's good. If my word counts, Chance is creepy but harmless. But he doesn't have to come with me either.

{inaudible}

You're sweet, but I'm ok. I will take one of those cigarettes, though.

*

That night, Officer Marona's dashcam only gets the basics. There is the hypnotic scroll of the highway centerline, a long tunnel of trees spreading out from the darkness, the twin beams from the cruiser painting briefly over Dale Perkins' mailbox. Then there's Marona walking around to let Dale Perkins' little brother out of the back seat, and, while he's occupied, a blur of movement on the porch behind him.

While reviewing the footage later on, Marona is pretty sure of three things. He's pretty sure the movement isn't Dale Perkins. In the grit of the footage, the guy is skinner, taller. There's a frame where the guy's eyes pick up the headlights, suspended in the gloom like a deer, like a ghost. He's pretty sure Dale Perkins' little brother sees the whole thing too, though at the time, the boy didn't say a word, just spat in the leaves when Marona asked if he had a key to get inside. He's also pretty sure the guy drops a bag, though it's hard to tell exactly if this is true given the angle of the camera. Something falls over the rail of the porch, landing in the hedge by the steps, a long strap hanging just in view.

Officer Marona gives some thought to that bag. He gives some thought to the ghost-man too, and to Dale Perkins, to his migrant work crews and his shirtless little brother tossing old eggs and baloney onto parked cars. He thinks of the blankness of the boy's eyes in his rearview mirror. He thinks of his daughter, scrolls through the empty inbox on his cellphone. Then he takes a cigarette from his drawer and chews the filter for a long time in the dark.

*

The manager of Morrison's Party Rentals tucks his wife into bed with the same routine every night. He brings her a glass of water, which she'll sip with each pill, and if she asks, he'll rub her neck with his thumbs, up to the soft spot behind her ears that he will later kiss when he comes to bed. He'll flip the white-noise machine on—a vestige of her time working night shift—and flip off the lights. Then he'll slide into bed and hold her body. His knees will fill the space behind hers, the noise machine whooshing softly. After a minute, he'll squeeze her, say *you're my love*. She'll reply *you're my love*, with a stress on the *my*, and he'll slide back out of bed, feeling the smile of her words.

Tonight, once he's finished, the manager heads down the stairs, through the kitchen and the lingering smells of hot-dish and old salad dressing. He takes the basement steps slowly, feels the air change as he gets to the bottom. The monitor of his desktop bathes his skin a deep blue. He pushes in the DVD from Morrison's security cameras, presses play.

Around his computer are stacks of library books—mysteries, mostly. The manager likes a good mystery. He feels like there's something comforting in their promise, in the way that the giddy chaos of their early plots eventually funnel into line.

On his screen, the vignettes in front of Morrison's flicker past, the time-stamp winding along in the right-hand corner. Headlights from cars exiting the parking lot at Parkview Baptist scroll past in the background.

The manager remembers how a pastor from a church he'd attended as a boy used to say, "it is God's will," when fielding impossible questions—why kids get cancer, why there is so much suffering in the world. Though he has long-since lost his faith, the manager remembers himself feeling jealous, a strange ache in his heart at the confidence of those words.

On the screen, a small figure, spray-can in hand, appears. The manager winds the video back and plays it again until the figure steps into the frame. Dale Perkins' brother, he guesses, though the boy is wearing something different this time. Something he recognizes. A spandex Spider-Man suit, fit for an adult but hanging off the boy's knobby frame, its skin webbed with red and black and blue.

Sometimes, after he's been drinking, he imagines a camera that has recorded his whole life—that has recorded all our lives. The camera has no blind spots, and it spares us none of the gritty minutia of our body's needs. It knows the meaning of our deeds and the truths of our hearts. He interrupts these thoughts often, but they return to him all the same, and like the parlor-scene at the end of one of his mysteries, they comfort him. Not with the truth, because he isn't sure he knows what that is. Not with answers, but with the possibility of their presence, of their infinite collection, saved up somewhere, just beyond his view.

When the Time Came

During the conversation with the police officer, Chester couldn't take his eyes off the doorway to the shed. He pictured the girl sitting in the dark, perhaps on the bottom step beneath the hatchway of the bunker. He pictured her pulling her shirt over her nose, adjusting to the bitter smell of moldy earth, the chill of the wet wood paneling, the dim glow from his old battery-powered Mickey Mouse nightlight that hung above the workbench. He'd unhooked the genny to mine it for parts, so if she tried the light switches she'd be disappointed. As the officer spoke, Chester felt a spasm of regret about the condition of the bunker, a quick tally of the unfinished projects that sat in systemless piles in the dark. Yet he could also feel the thunder of his own pulse. It was the strangest feeling, a thrill beyond anything he'd felt in years, and he could barely keep the words the policeman spoke in earshot, as if they were spinning away from him in the wind. He almost giggled when he replied. Simple sentences: *Yes sir. No sir. I will sir*. After a few minutes, a couple of state troopers appeared at the north end of the yard. They walked with Maglites pointed to the earth in slow steps, one smoking a cigarette that hovered in the twilight. The officer talking to Chester worked the gum in his mouth, turned away and spoke into his walkie-talkie.

"You keep a firearm in the house?" the office asked.

"Yes sir."

"Any other weapons on your property?"

"Just the twelve-gauge in the kitchen and the thirty-aught-six in the mudroom."

"Nothing out in the shed?" The officer's small eyes held Chester's for a moment before turning towards the cluster of outbuildings silhouetted beneath a stand of slash pine. Chester noticed the man's jaw had stopped moving.

"Tools, maybe," Chester said, the heat of his blood burning his skin from underneath. "Hatchet, a circle saw that doesn't work. No guns though."

The officer whistled at the two men searching the edge of the property line. He unhooked his own light from his belt and held it up to his shoulder, tapping his finger quickly on the button and sweeping the beam towards the shed. Then he turned back to Chester.

"Mind if we have a look anyway?" he asked, the words flat and formal, but carefully strung together, a pause hovering at the end.

Chester smiled weakly, rubbing the back of his neck as if it were sore. "Of course. I'll show y'all around."

*

The night before, Chester had woken in a sweat, his body still, the fan circling lazily above him in the dark. A memory was playing in his mind, or a piece of a memory, an afternoon conversation with a court-appointed counselor a year ago. It was the same afternoon his brother's trial had started, and he'd worn the closest thing he had to a suit to the appointment in the hopes of making it to the courthouse afterward. It had been a stifling summer, and he remembered the office where the interview took place—the low ceilings and cheap vinyl-wood paneling, the squeak of an air-conditioning unit in the high window along the wall. He'd answered a bunch of questions using a Scantron and a number 2 pencil, and the counselor had fed the sheet into a machine before turning to talk to him.

"Would you say you're a lonely man?" the counselor had asked.

"Wouldn't say it," Chester said.

"But you do prefer to be alone?"

"Can't be sure if I do," Chester said. "If T-Bob gets riled up I just leave him be. Usually take the dogs out to Broussard's pond."

"It's just you and Robert living at your property in Natchitoches?"

"Aint in Natchitoches proper," Chester said, "but yea. Just me and him."

"Does he drink a lot too?" the counselor asked.

Chester leaned his sweating, bulky back into the chair and tried to focus on the man in front of him. The counselor had a balding island that capped his salt-and-pepper hair, and Chester watched intently as the gossamer grey comb-over wiggled in the breeze of the AC vent. He thought of oyster grass, smelled his own heat in the chair.

"T-Bob's thing ain't to drink much," Chester said.

The counselor wrote something in his book.

"So you drink alone," he said, less a question than a statement.

"With the dogs, sometimes," Chester said.

"Had you been drinking alone the night Robert asked you to pick him up?"

"With the dogs, yea."

"Were you aware that your brother had assaulted a man before he called you that night?"

"I already talked to the cops about that," Chester said.

"Were you angry when he called you?"

"No."

"How did you feel when he called?"

Here, Chester felt the edges of his memory approach, like a fog filling the room from the corners. Soon, he and the counselor were haloed in the gloom, the words now uncertain but somehow feeling true, his lips moving in the bed in the dark.

"Nothing to feel. T-Bob calls me if he needs me and I come."

Then there was no more room. No counselor. Just the blades of the ceiling fan turning through stripes of moonlight from the shades.

"I don't know what to do now," he said to the fan. "With him gone, I don't know what to do."

*

The policemen stood behind Chester in the shed as he fumbled with the padlocks to the storage lockers. He opened up the empty chest freezer and they peeked inside, hands over their faces as if they expected rotten meat. He pushed aside a stack of PVC pipes T-Bob had cut for the bunker, opened the power tool closet and stood back to let the men by. One flicked the dead switch by the doorway.

"Genny's not working," Chester said apologetically.

One officer swung the beam of his flashlight overhead, the light dancing off the rusty ends of old tools. Static crackled on their radios, and outside the evening settled in with a pulsing rush of crickets.

"You recognize anything missing?" the officer with the chewing gum asked, playing his light along the workbench and back through the rafters.

"No sir," Chester said without looking. He took a step back, feeling the slight give of the metal bunker hatch hidden beneath the filthy strip of Astroturf laid out across the floor. He stood still and let the officers walk around him.

"Our suspect was armed during the robbery," the officer said, his hands playing along the stacked drawers marked *nails, brads, screws, nuts, washers.* Chester waited.

"If she tossed the weapon she'll be on the lookout for another," the officer continued, his eyes now on the light in Chester's kitchen window. Through the crickets, they heard the soft baying of hounds.

"She shoot someone?" Chester asked.

The officer spat his gum into the grass by the doorway. "Once we're done here, you'll want to account for your firearms in the house, sir. You'll also want to keep your floodlights on and the phone handy. If you see anyone on your property you are not to engage them. You are to call 911 immediately, is that understood?"

"She shot someone, huh?" Chester said, feeling a quick dizzy rush, like he'd stepped off a curb without looking. The heat beneath his skin returned. The officer looked at him, his face going flat for just a second. The hounds bayed. Then his radio sprang to life.

*

The bunker was T-Bob's plan. Most things were, as it turned out, but with the bunker project, some kind of urgency had taken hold of him that had been absent during their normal upkeep of the family property. Chester thought often about what it meant, this change, this fever that had seized T-Bob way back in the winter of 2005. He liked the purpose of things, that much he knew. The dog kennel project had been a disaster, and for all the talk about restoring their late father's Chevelle, they'd both let the thing go to rust on blocks underneath a boat tarp. A wildness had possessed T-Bob when he first returned from the work crews in Baton Rouge. His brother's intensity that winter felt strangely religious, and Chester remembered a sensation when his brother spoke about it, some kind of heat radiating from his limbs, sluicing down the networks of veins that emerged from blue tattoos like live electric wires. There were tent-camps, T-Bob said. There was army, National Guard, FEMA, and Red Cross. There were rumors of looting, a curfew run by the military, Humvees that scoured the neighborhoods at night with spotlights. T-Bob and many of the construction crews had been hustled out by the Humvees at twilight, past lines of trucks parked on lawns and guardsmen with rifles at sling-ready.

T-Bob had heard stories about the Superdome. New Orleans had burned and then drowned, he said, and Chester pictured the smoke above the water, rising in columns like the refineries that lit the marsh sky at night from Lake Charles to Beaumont. They'd emptied the whole city. A quarter million blacks, he said. On foot, in cars, spreading like an ash cloud north, east, and west.

The day after T-Bob returned from the work crews, he held a meeting with several folks whose property adjoined theirs. Chester had not been invited, but he watched through the kitchen window as the men talked in the yard. He recognized the Broussard brothers, and a guy that did oil changes at Phillips 66. Everyone was armed, everyone smoked. They pointed to various spots on the perimeter of the property, checked the chambers of their rifles, smoked some more, ground the butts into the soil with their work boots. That night, T-Bob sat down with Chester and told him about the plan for the bunker. He wanted it close by, but not a part of the house proper. It was something they would share with a few neighbors, something for when the time came. The Broussards had an excavator that they'd used for their pond. The oil-change guy was ex-military and had a line on surplus goods: ponchos, gaiters, MREs. T-Bob would skim construction materials at work and collect them for the bunker. The rest they'd purchase above board, a little at a time. When the hole was ready they'd build a toolshed above the entrance. They'd sink vent shafts. They'd keep records. They'd all pitch in.

In some way, Chester felt like there was a family being built on his property. It was a family in a grave, a family fed by cistern, a family tucked away beneath a toolshed like a happy secret. At night, once the bunker had been cleared and the shed was underway, he'd sneak out in the late hours, open up the hatch, step down into the hole and sit in the darkness. He'd listen to the wet earth breathe, watch the moonlight through the bare ribs of the unfinished shed roof. Sometimes he'd think of his parents, know that they were down here somewhere in the soil, and he listened for them, too.

*

The girl had appeared on his property when he was in the kitchen. Chester was putting the dog pills in peanut butter when the motion sensor lights tripped. The sun hadn't fully sunk, and he didn't see them at first. The pills kept breaking free, and his fingers were sticky. Through the window above his kitchen sink, two triangles of sodium-yellow flipped on, patterned with a black web of tree branches. He watched, waiting for the profile of a deer to emerge, or perhaps for the lights to simply click off.

Behind Chester, the dogs whined and scraped their paws on the linoleum. He waited so long that one of the dogs leaned in and bit the peanut butter pill ball out of his pudgy hand, gently but urgently. Chester swatted her muzzle, dropped the other pill ball, and by his feet, dog-tongues swiped the floor. He looked back out the window. For a moment longer, nothing. Then, just as the lights clicked off, a form—long blonde hair haloed in yellow, moving in a half-crouch towards the shed. He blinked.

*

The two state troopers were running back to their car, speaking excitedly into their walkie-talkies. Headlights came on, and one of the cars peeled out in a 180 down the driveway, red taillights bobbing through the trees. The officer Chester had spoken to seemed to hesitate, walking slowly and muting his radio each time a voice came on. Chester followed him out of the shed, though their path seemed to head more towards the house than to the driveway, where the officer's car was still parked. Above the treeline, the stars were already beginning to peek out. Chester still felt giddy, but also uncertain about what was happening. He knew he should be quiet, but his hand trembled at the thought of grabbing the officer's radio and listening in, piecing together the story as all these strange men with guns raced off in the dark towards some uncertain end. He thought of the army, of the police in military vehicles that T-Bob had talked about all those years ago. This time he saw them lined up along the road back to Natchitoches. They were fanning out in columns through the trees, dogs and flashlights prowling the underbrush, strobed from above by searchlights borne upon helicopters. He listened for the *chopchopchop*, for the dogs and men, but he only heard his footsteps and those of the officer and the returning static of the crickets in the trees. The officer stopped beneath the kitchen window.

"Sir, if you've seen anyone here tonight and not told us, you are obstructing a police investigation," the officer said, each of his words measured slowly, as if he were speaking to a child. "That is a crime. Do you understand that?"

Chester stood a few yards away in the shadows. He watched the girl in his memory. She'd been hurt, he could tell that as soon as he'd opened the shed door and found her. Her ankle was fat and turned a weird angle, and she winced when she shifted into a crouch, holding a hacksaw at him as he stood in the doorway. There had not been a gun. He watched her in his mind, and thought about his own stillness in that moment, hands at his sides, words that he didn't recognize percolating silently in his chest.

"Now, are you sure nobody's been through here?" the officer asked. His hand cupped his radio, his face inscrutable in the dark. Chester held the moment in his lungs like the first breath of a good cigarette. He pictured the girl's eyes when the red and blue lights had swept through the trees by the highway, watched them widen and glaze. It was a dead animal look, a thing on the threshold between flight and giving in. He imagined binding her ankle the way he'd seen T-Bob build a splint for his little cousin's broken arm. He imagined her walking the dogs with him down at Broussard's pond, imagined her handy with a wrench beneath the old Chevelle. He imagined her riding shotgun to pick up T-Bob at his release from prison.

"Sir?"

The girl had hesitated when he pointed at the bunker hatch cover, its metal edge protruding from beneath the Astroturf rug.

"Sir."

He didn't want the officer to leave. He realized this. He was trembling, the heat beneath his skin now gone. The longer the officer stayed, the longer they would each be suspended and together, the three of them, in something great and urgent and real. But the officer did not stay. The radio was chattering. Chester was shaking his head. And now the officer was already leaving, already pulling out of the drive, already disappearing into the gloom like a memory at the end of its tape. When he was gone, Chester would stand in the yard for a while, his head crowned in starlight. The hounds would moan from inside the house. The girl would sit underground, counting the silence. The words would stick and tumble, and he would stand in the doorway to the shed once again, practicing them in a whisper lost on the tide of crickets and the wind in the grass; *now you can go, now you can go, now now now.*

The Wick

1.

There was a moment, right before the man's plane hit the water, when time behaved strangely. That it did so didn't surprise him—he'd flipped in a canoe and nearly drowned as a boy, and his memory of the experience had been like a cascade of photographs spread out on a table, the details poking out at different angles each time he looked at them. His canoe had slipped over in less than a second, but he could still describe the halo of sun through the cypress boughs. The mulchy, bitter burn of duckweed in his nostrils. The tiger-striped legs of the banana spider he'd leaned over to avoid.

That he'd frozen up wasn't surprising either. Losing control of an aircraft was terrifying. He had earned his commercial license that same year, was still in his first month with the company, had rarely flown alone in foul weather. He'd only just registered the squawk of the stall warning when he was suddenly entombed in sound. The alarms overlapped in the cockpit, high and low, punctured by snare-drum bursts from Nassau Tower Approach, a thousand decibels pressed into a long, oscillating wail.

What surprised him was the clarity that came with the instant his plane crossed into an unrecoverable spin. This instant was a separate space. It was a wick of time that bridged the bracing with the letting-go, and he recognized it for what it was so intuitively that the noise and the lights and the chaos around him simply dropped out of view. And there, instead, was a time capsule he'd buried with his 3rd grade class. The kids had collected trinkets and toys, and with them, notes to their future selves. Some were lists of aspirations, crushes, catalogues of best-friends, and his, a confession that he'd triple-folded so that the teacher wouldn't be able to read it. The capsule was then sealed and buried beneath the garden behind the recess yard. Or perhaps, it was buried at sea. Or it was buried in the coal-colored water that was rushing up to meet him, for here was that capsule once again, opening from below, and within it an echo of many voices, one of which was his own.

2.

His confession: when he was young, he'd dream of erasure. Like walking without footprints across a wet concrete sidewalk, or leaving a crowded room without anybody noticing. Once he was alone he'd get lonely, and then he'd dream of warm returns, of clingy hugs from his mother and confidential admissions from the older kids in school that his absence was itself a presence, something that everyone felt, a cause for self-reflection and perhaps for more peaceful days on the playground. He wanted to be there but not be there. He wanted it both ways. Sometimes, while the cat prowled back and forth through the flap on the screen door, now inside, now out, he'd wonder if the ghosts of dead relatives watched over the spaces where they used to live. Then he'd stare long and hard at the high corners of the room and think twice about picking his nose.

3.

That cat was named Batman, born to a stray they'd given shelter to after his father left home. His mother had called the stray Miss Woo. She left bowls of water on the back porch, along with little cans of Fancy Feast that the roaches would swarm over at night, but Miss Woo was no more governed by Fancy Feast than she was by his mother's sing-song calls from the porch after dinner, *Miss Woo, Miss Woo, come home little girl.*

Batman was the sole survivor of the litter, and after she'd given birth, Miss Woo came less and less frequently, then seasonally, then not at all, until the boy and his mother would only imagine spotting her in the yard amongst the azaleas when the afternoon shadows spread across the garden. Batman fattened up, stalking roaches that slipped through the AC vents. The boy's mother gained weight too. She grew morose, rolled her own cigarettes and left the loose tobacco on the table. A carousel of men moved through her life, and the boy learned to avoid them by constructing routines, all of them little escapes that orbited further and further out before swinging back home.

4.

When the hurricane came they rode it out with Hugh, the man his mother was dating at the time. The boy liked Hugh. Hugh had skin the color and thickness of belt-leather, and had taken an early retirement to become a beekeeper. Together they had scaled the eaves and gutters of the house, wiring storm shutters closed and cross-taping windowpanes. From the roof they watched a parade of cars heading out Carrolton Avenue towards I-10. Hugh let the boy take drags on his cigarette until the first squall-lines rolled over the city and the cars dissolved into a winding red glowworm in the dark.

That night they sat in the living room, next to a canoe that Hugh brought over from his place. Hugh told a story about paddling on the Big Bouge Chitto, about the river coming up suddenly in the night, about hitching his boat to the trunks of trees as black water hissed and sucked through the branches all around him. The boy's mother told Hugh to stop scaring everybody. The power went out. The house moaned. The boy held Batman in his lap, sitting cross-legged in the bow of the canoe, feeling the claws knead his skin in the dark, little flashes of pain that bobbed like lights on a dark ocean.

The next morning they inspected the damage. A tree was down, some shingles had peeled off the roof, but the house was intact. They grilled all the meat from the freezer, and they burned deadfall in the backyard while Hugh played The Everly Brothers on his harmonica. The following morning they saw smoke on the horizon. The fridge had started to sour, and when he hauled the garbage to the curb, the boy heard little firework pops on the breeze. The water came that afternoon. It was slow, a lava-flow that crept up Carrolton from the lake, swallowing front lawns and politely collecting garbage as it came.

There was panic and indecision in the house. Hugh wouldn't leave. The boy's mother stacked furniture into towers, grabbed a milk-crate of photo albums, and got the jeep started as water pooled in the drive. They couldn't find the cat. The boy called and called. He tossed the house searching, but the yard was already filling up, and Hugh finally pulled him off his feet and carried him to the jeep. Hugh said it would be alright. He said he would find Batman. He said he would keep the house safe, pulled a .38 from the back of his waistband and waved it in the direction of the highway, smiling. Hugh stayed on the lawn, ankle-deep, until the boy and his mother drove off. They drove with the water at their heels, followed the river to the Crescent City Connection, and then out through Bridge City, Avondale, and the rusty clay high-ground of Baton Rouge.

5.

They never saw Hugh again, but he wrote them a letter, addressed to the boy's mother at her sister's house in Shreveport two months after the storm. The water peaked at five feet at the house. The looters never came. Hugh was picked up by the National Guard, though he'd pleaded for more time to find the cat. They took him to a camp—just a row of tents in a parking lot up by Tickfaw—but he landed with a volunteer crew doing house-to-house searches in the city soon after. Unbelievably, when he returned to the house he found Batman there, just a sack of bones at thatpoint, mewing on the steps by the porch. He took the cat and nursed it back to health, kept it with him in Tickfaw and then Hattiesburg. Batman had been happy, Hugh said. He was grateful, always close underfoot, even sleeping on the bed at night until he escaped out an open window one morning and was run over by a car. The letter concluded with an apology to the boy, and an address for correspondence to the boy's mother. Below the last typed line he'd scribbled *there is a home for all lost things* in a strange, sloping cursive.

By then, however, the boy's father had re-entered the picture. He was living with them in Shreveport, and after a cookout one evening the boy watched his mother slip out the back door and burn the letter on the grill.

6.

Many years later, and a month before his pilot's exam, his father called out of the blue to talk about a Pete Seeger guitar lick he'd once learned but now couldn't quite remember. It *went wana wana wana wah*, his father said, knocking his fingertips on the receiver of the phone in little pops. His father had been drinking, ignoring doctor's orders about his upcoming surgery, and in his indirect way, he was calling to tell his son something else. He kept with the *wana wana wanas*, saying *you know the one right, you know the one*, until his son finally said *I know it, yea*, and then they each listened to the fingertips tapping the receiver, in even beats now like the clip of tires on concrete seams on a long, straight highway.

7.

After he passed his pilot's exam, he drove back down to New Orleans. His father was in hospice there, but the caretaker said he was sleeping and unable to take visitors. Unsure of what else to do with his afternoon, the man holed up in a bar until he couldn't drive himself home. Sometime later, a guy in a sweat-soaked linen suit came in and sat down. The guy's fingers did a spider-walk on the bartop while waiting for his scotch, and it dawned on the man that he knew him somehow. His name was Garret, or Garth, or something with a G, the older brother of a classmate, though he seemed decades older now, whittled down and sharp at the corners. Eventually they shared a cigarette outside, and while G exhaled, his eyes seemed to rest on the man for the first time, enough so he knew that he knew him. They shook hands. They asked sincere-sounding questions, and now loosened up, they followed each other back inside with the fuzzy glow of alcohol spreading warmly around the room.

G did most of the talking. He said that he'd been a photographer with the Picayune when the hurricane came. He'd stayed in town through the storm, slept on porches, shot pictures of the dead and the not-quite-dead. The day after landfall, he'd linked up with a pair of staffers from the paper living out of a news van. They tailed national guardsmen, siphoned gas from cars, slept in shifts. There was a features editor, an older woman with sandy blonde hair who ran ultramarathons, who left for New York City soon after G joined them. The other staffer was a creole, barely old enough to keep a beard, who, like G, was also a photographer.

A week after landfall, up near St. Claude, the creole had found a teenager carrying two liters of tonic water over his shoulders. Following the boy's directions, he came to a flooded corner store with the words *Looters Will Be Shot* spray-painted across the plywood covering its windows. The creole took photos there as people came and went, including a picture of an elderly black man ferrying a case of ramen noodles on his head. Later, this picture appeared in a newspaper story about looting. He hadn't used the word, but there it was, once in orange letters across the window-boards, and now atop the headline as if he'd written it himself. He tried writing an editorial to explain that, like the man in his photo, he and G had lived for nine days off of supplies they'd scavenged from the city, but this was a time when nothing and everything was true. This was when the cops were ferrying survivors to shelter, when they were shooting people and burning their bodies in the trunks of cars. The levees had been bombed, the president was in on it, and everyone lucky enough to be outside of the city was desperate for an answer that made sense, that let them change the channel before they'd lost hope entirely.

G sucked the ice from his scotch. The creole had a hard time for a while, he said, but eventually settled down in the area. He'd bought a house on the north shore, married a girl from Rhode Island. G paused, and music from the speakers revved up overhead. Then, in the flat cadence of a pilot walking through his pre-flight checks, he said that the creole's wife had come home last weekend to find him locked in the garage with the windows up and the car running. G sort of laughed, expelling all his air in a puff, his mouth hanging slightly open afterwards like he was waiting for someone else to pick up where he left off.

8.

Later, at his hotel, the man finished all of his cigarettes and then scrubbed the space between his fingers with soap. He hadn't really wanted to hear G's story. He hadn't asked. And because he hadn't asked, he'd let the silence that followed it stretch out until the winds of the evening shifted, until the lights of G's cellphone danced on the glass of his eyes, until a cab arrived and he made his exit with a soft, apologetic squeeze of the man's shoulder.

The man spoke to the mirror about what he would've said, what he would have told G if he'd been asked. He tried out some words about Hugh, but couldn't get past the part about the cat. Who cared about a fucking cat? Who cared that his mother got back together with his father, or that everyone had always treated this fact like a reprieve for which he'd never been properly grateful? Surely no one could keep tallies so small.

That night in bed, he looked back at those hours following the storm as if they'd known the water was coming. Before they'd shuttered the windows, before he sat with Hugh on the roof and watched the exodus of the willing and able, he'd felt the wall of rain on its way. Every minute of their lives had been a story of that creeping tide, of its inevitability, of its terrible slowness.

9.

Eleven months later, while on a layover in Lake Charles, he visited New Orleans for the last time. He was due in Ft. Lauderdale the next evening, then on to Nassau, but he rented a car anyway and kept the thunderheads over the gulf on his right as he drove. He made it to the city by sunset, coming in across the Bonnet Carre Spillway with the tops of oil towers flickering fire-orange in the distance.

He parked outside of the old house and sat there in the dark. The lawn where Hugh had stood, pistol in hand, waving them away in the morning sunshine had been dug up and re-planted. Once a simple plot of Bermuda grass, now beds of amaranth, nightshade, spider lilies. A sapling cyprus grew from the garden's edge, sheltering the glow from the living room windows. He saw children's toys scattered on the porch steps—masked crime fighters, sidewalk chalk, a remote-control dune buggy. Inside, someone was tinkering on a piano.

He listened to the engine tick, slowing as it cooled, until the evening had settled to a stop around him. Departure was at dawn, but there was no rush. The moon crested the eaves of the house. Junebugs tumbled and scuttled on the windshield. He held this stillness close to him, unwilling to move, imagining that when the moment finally felt right, when the air in the car smelled of pollen and rainwater and a familiar, blossoming rot, he would open the door.

Homecoming

Etienne wouldn't see the sharks so much as feel them. A quick, hard tug, then slack again. He would look back at the polymer-coated wire that ran from a loop around his waist through the quaking necks of drum and speckled trout he'd caught, trailing outward behind his body in the water like an s-curved tail, its tip a white foam buoy glazed brown with salt and sparkling in the afternoon sun. The tide was leading the stringer behind him, and the backs of the fish he'd caught swished and boiled against the surface. There would be a tug, sometimes two, but rarely a splash. The buoy would sink to its fat midriff, tremble, and then bob up again, jaunty and slick.

When his father had lifted him out of the boat, he'd been terrified. He slid down to a standing position in the water, his feet lost in the deep green beneath him. He could only feel the sand through his shoes, the caress of the current, the cool-to-warm settling of the water on his skin. The waves came to his chest and slapped against the hull of the boat. He was eye-level with the rail, the metal gunnels flecked with fish blood, the white resin surface stained along the waterline. His father was haloed by the sun, an angular shadow rocking above him, hair radiating like fire in the wind.

Remember to shuffle your feet when you walk, his father said.

I will, Etienne said.

If you don't, you'll step on a sting ray. They'll get out of the way if you shuffle.

I'll remember, Etienne said.

Then his father nodded at Gil Delacambre, who started the outboard. A cloud of diesel spun in the wind, and the boat motored off to the east, smaller and smaller, until the boy could only hear the soft put put put and the water licking against the fabric of his T-shirt.

In every direction, Etienne saw color. Coal-blue waves rippling in the summer wind, a white dome of sky patterned with cotton, mirage-haze at the horizon and oil rainbows that coiled and slid past him on the water's surface. He was simply a boy standing in the sea, impossibly here, on two feet, and now alone. Here there was the Gulf of Mexico and the sky and nothing else. For five minutes, he panicked. He peed, felt the warmth on his thighs and then the cold creeping back. There was no land in sight. He couldn't see the island they'd set up camp on, a spit of crushed shells and sand in the barrier group by Breton Sound, its white dunes peppered with oyster grass that nudged only six inches above the waterline. He closed his eyes. He felt the salt wind, the gooseflesh, then a gradual evening out of his heartbeat. He thought of how his body would adjust like this in cold swimming pools on boiling afternoons back in New Orleans. *Ok*, he said to the wind. Then he checked the gill string, unhooked his lure from the tip of his spinner rod, and tossed it out into the waves.

*

The park ranger is telling the sheriff's man and a couple of local reporters that Etienne's father may have had a death wish. This strikes Etienne as wrong, but nonetheless he considers it. At 30, he has come to understand the term in a detached, third-person kind of way, precise in how it describes people who are only characters to him. BASE jumpers and daredevils on TV. Soldiers who sign up for repeat tours overseas. Adventurers in airport novels. He calls upon these images to make a subtle demarcation between the idea of people who provoke death, poking its den with a stick to see when it will come hissing after them, and people like his father. It seems an unfair term here, yet maybe they are right. Etienne's father is now 74 years old, with two bad shoulder sockets and a back that seizes daily until he lies down to stretch. He is active for 74, but this is the kind of mixed blessing that has already fueled speculation about his state of mind.

Had his father been arrogant, paddling out into the swamp with a backpack, a sandwich, a pair of water bottles? No phone or emergency kit. No life jacket even. He'd been doing this for decades, since his children were old enough to kneel in the canoes with him, to play with GI Joes and watch the morning steam lift off the water under the unrelenting southern sun. The man was a veteran. Military survival training, trips to the Arctic Circle, the Wind River Mountains, the steep basalt canyons of the Pacific Northwest . Etienne's mother had said once that he was born in the wrong century, and as a boy, Etienne had latched onto that idea with some sense of pride. A caveman father. A frontiersman in a wetland that sinks further and further into history. Arrogant, maybe. But for Etienne, arrogance doesn't fully square with a man who had a death wish. What is arrogant about a suicide? Moreover, what is a suicide without a body?

Etienne stands at the boat ramp and watches the assembled group of volunteers drink cold coffee from a thermos, talking and swatting mosquitoes. It's day two of the search, and everyone's face has the same flat composure. It looks a lot like boredom, but Etienne knows better, has seen that look from cops in the city. The only exception is the ranger, a woman in her mid-40s with hair the deep tea-color of creekwater, graying in stripes that almost flash in the sun. She is clouded with gnats, but there's a liveliness in her gestures when she talks to the reporters. Her hands are on her hips now, eyes looking back towards the darkening shapes of cypress that border the edge of the Atchafalaya Wildlife Refuge. Etienne follows their gaze to the trees, to the deep spaces between them that echo with crickets and cicadas and tree frogs. A white noise hums steadily during breaks in the conversation, swelling up through the pauses all at once, holding everyone momentarily in the sound of a freefall.

*

Like most childhood memories, the memory of the fishing trip in Breton Sound is so imprecise that Etienne discovers that he's changed details each time he recalls it. Sometimes he can still see the boat while he's wading in the gulf, sometimes he's abandoned all on his own. Sometimes he sees a shark hit his stringer, sometimes he just feels the tug on the line and pees himself, too scared to look back, counting the seconds until the line around his waist goes slack again. He can't recall if Gil Delacambre stays overnight with them on the island, or if he simply drops them in the evening and returns the next day. It is 30 miles back to the marshes along Louisiana's crumbling edge, so it seems unlikely that Gil would've left and returned, but Etienne can't picture the boat in the surf, the man's tent, anything about his presence that night on the island. He can picture the thunderheads at sunset, white cliffs descending into a reddish haze below, grinding inexorably closer from the south. He remembers the halo of sun in his father's hair from up in the boat when he drops him in the water. He remembers a flash of teeth, like a smile, before the motor revs to life.

*

His father had brought the dog with him. Five days ago now, in the morning, he'd strapped the old fiberglass canoe to the roof of the jeep, singing a little song as he helped the dog climb into the passenger seat. The dog was fourteen, and more visibly hobbled by age than Etienne's father had ever shown himself to be. She was a mutt of the swamp. His father had found her on a canoe trip with his students, pulled her tiny form from a spit of land at the edge of Bayou Sauvage, wrapped her in his T-shirt, and left her on his lap the whole drive home. At first he was just going to clean her up before putting her up for adoption. Then he was just going to make sure she was inoculated and healthy. Then it had to be the right owner, someone he could trust with the dog, not just some asshole who would tie her up in the yard and leave her there. Eventually, she just became their dog, without anyone saying so out loud. The situation just settled, like sediment in the water, until everyone saw it clearly and nobody felt it could be any other way.

Etienne is having coffee with the park ranger, whose hair is pulled into a ponytail and whose hat rests on the table next to her walkie-talkie. The café is a few miles up from the boat launch where the search is being organized. There, a thinner group of volunteers, quieter each day, are eating brownbag lunches in the shade. There he'd caught whispers of things he'd rather not hear. Strangely, this hadn't angered him so much as made him pity the men and women who were searching for his father. He'd feel their eyes on him when he moved through the sphere of their conversations, felt them bite their tongues and clip the sharper edges of their doubts until he moved out of earshot again. He wanted to hold their hands and tell them not to hold back, but in his head this had sounded disrespectful, like he was picking a fight. Maybe the park ranger had sensed something, asked him to lunch to get away. Maybe she just pitied him. Maybe she has brought him here to give him the "realistic expectations" speech.

"It's not a suicide," Etienne says, breaking the silence filled by the trailing end of a song from the kitchen radio. The ranger looks out the window and then back over at him. Her face is taut and tired-looking. Her eyes are a deeper brown, almost black, wet and gilded with moons of refracted neon from the overhead.

"I suspect you don't want it to be," she says evenly, "but if we don't find him soon this is going to move to recovery. And honestly, it might be easier to view it that way."

Etienne thinks about this, about what choice was easiest for framing the loss of his father.

"It's not a suicide because he brought the dog," he says.

She straightens her back and sighs. "The dog does give him a much better chance of being found." She looks back out the window again, her eyes still caught with that look he'd seen three days ago with the reporters. Active. Thinking. She is the last holdout.

"I mean, he wouldn't kill the dog," Etienne says. "Intentionally, at least, he wouldn't put her in harm's way. If he'd meant to die, he'd have gone alone."

"You said the dog was old too," the ranger says. Etienne finds himself annoyed by the pragmatism in the ranger's suggestion.

"He found her in the swamp," Etienne says. "Rescued her from an island, probably a day or two from starving. Nursed her back. There's no way he'd do that."

"Was the dog sick?"

"Yes, but find a 14 year old dog that isn't."

A long pause, punctuated by the start-up of brass music from the kitchen and the clanging of silverware to the beat.

"Maybe he was taking her home," she says.

"I don't believe that," he says.

She holds his eyes with hers, their hands both on the table, fingertips separated by a narrow strip of lacquered wood like a channel. After an extended silence, the radio next to her warbles and then comes to life.

*

That night on Breton Island, the storm had broken with such fury that they could hear alarms going off on the oil rig whose lights danced in the distance to the east. Etienne imagined all the roughnecks evacuating, sliding down fire poles and cargo nets into waiting coast guard ships. They were leaving him, he thought. He'd wished that they could call the rig, tell them a man and his boy were on the island. Just so they would know, so it wouldn't be a mystery when the gulf rose up and swallowed them without a trace.

Out of the south, from a blackness strobed with lightning, a wind came up across the island with the force of a steam engine. He could hear the sand blasting the fabric of the tent, and he huddled close to his father, who lay with his back to the windward side, headlamp and reading glasses on, narrating Huckleberry Finn with a deep southern twang.

Golly, Huck, his father said, *if he a man, then why don't he talk like a man?*

At that moment, the tent came down around them, pressing them into the sand and dragging them along the dune. The light went out. They both gripped the ground through the fabric, searching for the rootstalks of oystergrass. He was screaming, deafly in the rush, and he held his father's shoulders, still bone and cartilage, still solid, still anchored to the earth.

*

The dog is at the boat launch. Surrounded by volunteer searchers who offer her bites of peanut butter sandwich es, she is turning in circles in the hot sun. She drinks from a bowl set down by someone, and then turns back to the treeline and whines, licking her muddy chops. Her fur is thickly woven with brambles and thorns. The volunteer who found her is an elderly, long-boned woman named Nelta who owns a gas station in Picayune. Nelta used to help Etienne's father run the shuttle back when his family canoed the creeks of southern Mississippi. She knows the dog by name, sits by her and runs her fingers through the matted fur, whispers *Good Bear, what a good girl, what a good good girl.*

Etienne is standing just outside the passenger door of the ranger's Jeep, shifting his weight from leg to leg, his pulse racing. Beneath his feet, the crushed oyster shells that pave the drive down to the boat ramp crackle and pop. Around him, several volunteers hover in a semi-circle. All of them are upbeat. Several conversations are going at once. A middle-aged guy in hunting camo and a blaze-orange penny stands next to Etienne smoking a menthol in long drags and nodding. "Had one like that when I was a boy," he says, to no one in particular, the words uncoiling in white puffs from his sunburned lips.

"It's an excellent sign," the ranger is saying, handing a laminated map to Nelta for her to examine. Etienne watches the sunlight on the ranger's hair, imagines some change in color that is seeping in now, turning tea to amber and amber to gold. Nelta has one hand anchored firmly on the dog, who has now laid down at the edge of the launch, panting and running her tongue along her nose. Etienne watches Nelta's hand work the dog's fur. He pictures his mother, thinks of that same casual movement of the fingers, of the claim her hands would lay. This came during silent afternoons on the back porch, a hand on the dog, the sun-baked smells of autumn drifting lazily over the town. It came during lowlight nights in the living room, during mornings in the kitchen with breakfast-crumbed fingers dragging low for curious noses to find.

Etienne knows, quite suddenly, that his father is dead. As clearly as he now tastes the diesel on the air, he knows it in a way that feels almost transcendental. He can see his father. It is yesterday, and he is many miles to the northeast, in a clearing between cypress knees, lying in the shade. The canoe is missing. He has his leg bound with the torn sleeves of his sweatshirt, the short spare paddle for a brace. He has made a fire. He always makes fires, but this one is a small one, and he is out of matches, and he is watching the light through the trees with the knowledge that another night out in the swamp will likely be his last. He is talking to the dog, pointing her southward across the wide inlet which they've paddled, towards the distant high ground that eventually links up to Route 105. He is whispering in his sing-song voice, cajoling her. He keeps pointing and clapping, go go go he says, but she won't go. She won't go until later, when it's dark and the ground comes alive with fire ants and stick-bugs and the wild night chorus of the sinking world. When he is no longer clapping and his skin has turned the coolness of the water. When enough time has passed for her to know that he won't whisper anymore, she will sniff the ground around him, turn in circles, lick his eyelids, and then turn uncertainly to where the inlet meets the land.

*

He'd awoken to the sound of gulls. The wet fabric of the tent lay pressed to their backs, filtering the light of morning into a pale red glow patterned with shadow droplets that slid and shimmered on their skin. Etienne had been asleep, although he didn't know how or when it had happened. Next to him, his father lay pressed into a depression in the sand, the folds of their collapsed tent obscuring his brow and part of his torso. Etienne could smell his breath, the unbrushed teeth and nighttime-dose of whiskey, and watched the air from his father's lips move the loose pages of Huckleberry Finn. Outside, the oyster grass tickled the tent walls in the wind. The air hummed. The gulls cackled. Etienne kept still, long past when his body began to ache with the need to stretch, to go pee, to unfurl the wet plastic from their backs and step out to see what the storm had done to the island. One of his hands still clutched the sand through the groundcloth, and as the sounds of the world crept in around him, he stayed still, strangely certain above all things that he would stay this way, unmoving, until his father stirred.

Apocrypha

High Ground

It was a misunderstanding of plate tectonics that did it. The models he'd seen in middle school: baking soda volcanoes bubbling over and swaths of clay that rolled along a layer of orange marbles, their edges sliding and buckling against each other. All of it terrified him, this testimonial tableau to the dynamism at work under our feet, belying the steadiness of solid words like "rock" and "ground" with ideas like "molten" and "convection." When his parents buried his pet guinea pig behind the house he'd cried, but less because he'd missed the guinea pig (a girl his father had named Jeffrey) than because he knew the moving earth would steal her. He pictured the time-lapse flow of the soil underneath his yard, taking up the animal's bones in its slow current and pulling them away southward, down the street towards the neighbors' yard, collecting the skeletons of cats and dogs and other sunken things. Eventually they would slip beyond the ocean shore. They would gather the rusting hulks of ships and the rings and shoes of lost sailors in their wake, spilling over an abyssal cliff to be recycled into carbon and lost to history.

The city the boy grew up in was 27 feet below sea level. On clear days he could watch the tanker ships churn slowly upriver above the eaves of houses along the levee. He'd learned that the river used to flood this region. He'd read about the natural processes that fed the marshes, about the river spilling tides of sand and silt swept down from Iowa, Oklahoma, Missouri. He knew there had been a great flood once back in the '20s, when no boats were there to save the people two-by-two, when good and wicked men drowned together. Their bodies had joined the emptied graves from the towns upriver, a spilled toy chest of corpses on the move, settling in trees and gutters and backroads before sinking inexorably back into the ground. His parents told him this wouldn't happen again. Great dams and channels had been built, highways for the water that let the ships float skyward past the treetops of town. He listened to the low echo of their bellowing horns on foggy nights, and dreamed of mumbling giants that coasted on the air.

In one story, he goes on to a science school but studies books. He works a side job bartending for day laborers caked in drywall and asbestos powder. He takes notes about the weird ones, makes friends with the guitarist who does Civil War reenactments, writes stories and finds his way back to school, again and again and again, until he's teaching some version of the few books he knows to students who don't know any books at all. Maybe there's a book in it for him too, one his father reads in his twilight years before canoeing out into the swamp one morning and never coming back. Maybe he keeps the letter his father sent about it locked in a box locked in his desk. Something too painful to read but totemic in its power. Maybe this moves him to some downshift, a spiral away from writing and into a gray space of life where the years slip away as easily as the crumbling marshlands he grew up in. Or maybe this moves him upward, a little powerhouse in his chest that explodes in white silence while he writes and writes and writes.

In another story he goes to that scientist school and learns science. He interns at the Hubble Space Telescope Observatory just north of campus, the same plot of ground he'd pilfered Christmas trees from as an undergraduate with his drunken roommates. He learns to see numbers as the pixels in a large, out-of-focus photograph. He learns he can zoom out until he sees the full picture, the widest operation of its grand and beautiful mechanics. He discovers a comet, gets a medal. A few weeks after retirement, his comet makes another pass through the neighborhood and strikes the southern polar surface of Mars, and the crater becomes his namesake. When he dies, his ashes make the final cargo manifest for the Mars Polar Excavator, and he is catapulted away, the clouds and deltas and shifting soils of home dwindling away beneath him in a long rocket trail.

Hardy

When the heart attack struck, Chet Morton was in his parents' basement watching a documentary about American explorers in the Patagonia. On the TV there was a pair of middle-aged men in a sailboat. Their skin was the color of red Mississippi clay, their silhouettes framed against a rocking sea and white-filtered peaks from another world. But it was this world, Chet knew. It was a world he had seen so much of while in the wake of the Hardy brothers, back in the days when he pictured himself in silhouette too, against Mayan temples and the cliffs of Arctic glaciers. Not long after those days had ended—after Joe and Biff moved west together and Frank lost his leg in the car accident—Chet had taken to looking back at himself with a romantic notion. He'd been less a sidekick than a gentleman scientist, he imagined. He'd been a polymath whose support was indispensable to the missions the Hardys had taken on. The stories he now told at the gun club became more and more centered on his role in the adventures they'd had together, on the ways in which his microscope had cracked a case or his skill with the boomerang had saved the day.

But a thought percolated in his mind during those stories. It was a whisper he heard over his own voice somehow, like a soft echo in a large room. He'd never really been afraid, the whisper said. Was it true? Even when he was tied up at gunpoint, when imprisoned in the cellar of an abandoned windmill, when careening towards a cliff in a driverless car—he'd felt it. There was some sense of calm, some trust. Chet wasn't a particularly spiritual man, less so after the Hardys' acrimonious split-up and the general, aimless decline his own life had taken since. No, it wasn't God turning the wheel of that car. But Chet realized that he was almost expecting it to happen. He'd felt the balance tip, the wheels run rough across the gravel shoulder and then glide out over the void, and he'd smiled. It seemed ridiculous, but he'd smiled. And right then, sitting on the couch in the basement with the sun-bronzed men in their sailboat casting TV whites and blues across the dark corners, when his arm began to tingle and go numb, he breathed deeply and closed his eyes, and he felt his nerves begin to leave his body, searching outward like roots in the air for the rescue he knew was coming.

Charlie

At the sound of approaching footsteps, the fox gave up on the leg and made away with the baby's left foot. She hadn't done the digging to get to the child's body, but she wasn't above taking the opportunity that presented itself. The bones separated a little too easily in the fox's mouth, the tissue soft and long-spoiled. The May morning air was chilly, and dew hung heavy in the low underbrush. The fox smelled the scent of dogs in the soil. One had marked the tree by which the body had been buried. Heavy work boots were marching now across the carpet of leaves, but the fox was already out of sight. She watched the outline of a man appear, stop next to the grave, put its hand on its hips, rub its strange head. Then she ran.

*

"I vividly remember being in Queens," Charlie is saying. "I was told in Sicilian that the kidnappers would kill me, and then there was a long period of living in warehouses. In the backs of pickup trucks covered in canvas. I didn't have a lot of other memories until I was a bit older."

Reporters crowd around him, snapping pictures and holding out voice-recorders. They make a motley group, maybe a dozen strong, strolling in slow steps across a gravel path that bisects a perfectly sheared lawn. Charlie's third wife cups her hand around the inner crook of his elbow, her smile persistent, her fingers pulling the thin cotton fabric of his sleeve into a pinched nexus of folds. The sun is unusually hot for this early in the year, and everyone is sweating a little. A scattershot of thin white clouds drift lazily overhead.

"What can you remember about your childhood?"

"Where did the kidnappers take you?"

"Did you ever try to escape?"

He surveys the reporters for a minute. There are fewer than he'd hoped for, fewer than he'd promised his wife. But he nods at each question as if he's complimenting the quality and precision of their nature, addressing them in turn with a well-practiced drop in baritone that his wife called "his serious voice."

"It's mostly fragments until we settled in Sacramento," he says, "though we stayed in Kansas with Al Capone's crew for several years after the kidnapping, all the way through the trial. I suppose my captors still hoped to broker a deal with my parents, but the media was too heavily involved. There wasn't any way to make contact without something leaking. Plus there were all the hoaxes and the grafters—that con man P.I. they eventually put behind bars. But you have to understand: I was a boy, and I was living with bootleggers and criminals. I had to ingratiate myself to them somehow. I learned to sew, to cook pasta, things like that. At some point I suppose it was all I knew. As it weird as it sounds, I didn't think about running. Not until much later."

*

"I can't say for sure," Charlie's psychiatrist, Dr. Mylen Fitzwater, says to an *L.A. Times* reporter in the dark of his living room. "But he honestly believed it was the truth. He was very consistent in what he said under hypnosis. He had a lot of very interesting details."

"Did you think he was delusional or paranoid?" the *L.A. Times* man responds. "Did you give him a diagnosis of some kind that might explain all of this?"

"I wasn't asked to give a diagnosis," Dr. Fitzwater says, huddling into his coffee.

"Maybe Charlie had a difficult life and saw an alternate identity as a means of escape," the reporter says.

Dr. Fitzwater places his coffee down and looks across the living room at the reporter. "He was functioning. He wasn't depressed or psychotic. He was just this fellow. This fellow who had this story he really wanted to get out."

*

"How does it feel to finally be home?" a reporter asks, holding out a device for Charlie to respond into. He looks at the device, weighing the tone of the reporter's question.

"I've yearned for years to return here."

"How do you feel about the Lindbergh's donation of Highfield to the state of New Jersey?" the same reporter asks.

There is a second where the words don't register, followed by a little thrill of electricity in his stomach. To his consternation, Charlie isn't ready for this question. He feels his wife's hand tighten on his arm. He senses her gaze turning to the manor home behind her, tracing the painted eaves and weathered brickwork. The estate looks manicured but empty. He'd assumed it had been made into a museum, or perhaps designated as a historical site. He can sense their doubt suddenly, like he is watching them sniff at the changing of the wind, but his mouth is already moving to respond.

"Our estate is in lovely shape," he begins. "The curators have done a wonderful job with it."

There is a pause in the interview, some nervous coughing.

"This is a juvenile rehabilitation center," the reporter says flatly. Cameras click and whirr.

*

The truck driver's name was William. He'd just finished urinating in the bushes when he saw the grave. He saw the trailing end of the leg, the joint where animals had severed the foot. He could smell it too. In fact, he'd smelled it first, and now his urine was soaking quickly into the ground 3 feet from the corpse, this tiny little thing, ribboned flesh mixing with bits of clothing, all blackened except for the white scrap of bone beneath freshly pawed dirt.

William did not think about rewards. He did not dig up the missing boy, he did not call the Lindberghs, or the media, or try to get his name in the papers. Instead, he smoked a cigarette slowly, watching insects land on the leg and waiting for his hand to stop shaking. Then he walked back to his truck, drove into town, and called the police.

*

The *L.A. Times* reporter is standing in the shade of a pine grove, sunshine filtering through the boughs in columns that catch the spring pollen in the air like glitter. He is shaking the hand of an ancient man in a blazer and polo shirt, a retired FBI agent from the New Jersey field office. The reporter is turning back towards the county road where his car is parked, when the FBI man speaks to him one last time.

"He's a fraud," the FBI man says. "He's an opportunist, a gun-nut, and a John

Bircher."

*

William read later in the papers that the autopsy on the boy was done quickly; a massive skull fracture and that was it. Afterward, the body was hastily removed from the coroner's office and cremated by the Lindbergh family. It bothered him to read this—the cremation part. It seemed like a second death, in ignominy equal to the first, this secret burning of what remained of the little boy. He'd been hunting with his grandfather in the boundary waters when he was younger, and he'd known something of the hunger with which nature reclaimed the dead. He'd spent one summer checking on the butchered carcass of a deer, a half mile from his uncle's cabin, its body already blackened and ruptured when he found it. He'd made up reasons to run off into the woods all summer long, watching in brief visits, in stop time, as the body attenuated, then flattened, then sank slowly beneath the autumn foliage that had begun to drop. He'd talked to the deer sometimes, a fact he'd never admitted to his grandfather or anyone else afterward. But it had felt like the right thing to do. To keep it company. To witness its burial into the bosom of a world that lovingly ate the creatures it made.

For the rest of his life, he dreamed of those woods in the boundary waters. In them, he was a boy without feet, wandering from lake to lake on the back of a deer, listening to the wild calls of the dead and the living on the night wind.

Last Note From the Dystopian Commune

He'd had a birthday party once, one of those parties which relied upon the industry of adults, and he'd dreaded its approach like the side-lit evenings of August and back-to-school clothing sales on the television. With months to go he started dropping hints of his concern. *I never want a big wedding* he'd stated absurdly one afternoon while his mother was toasting granola on the stovetop. She frowned and added more raisins. A week later he'd told his father he no longer wanted an ice cream cake. It was a lie—he loved ice cream cake—but it seemed suddenly fraught with logistical danger, this melty, urgent thing. He pictured three blobs on bright plastic plates and his parents on the far side of an empty dinner table, urging him to eat quickly. The final days had tightened around him in a knot. He found himself lying to his friends at school—even the kids he didn't know, the sixth graders who spent recess by the dumpster and watched glassy-eyed while he and his friends played monsters and heroes. *My birthday is actually in the summer*, he'd said, *my parents lied so I could stay a grade ahead*. The night of the party he faked a stomach ache and hid in his room.

*

It is late morning now, and he is sitting in the sun at the edge of the porch. The compound is empty, and a quiet heat has descended upon him, holding him in reverie. There is a bandage on his foot that pulses with his heartbeat. Flies hover around his foot, and he is thinking about the voices he felt he'd heard the night of that birthday, so long ago, murmuring outside the door of his room. Had there been voices? He'd had pillows pressed to his ears, and he remembers the close and quiet rush that purred while he held them there. Still, there were echoes of something else too, he was sure of it. Maybe his parents, knocking on his door. Maybe the throng of his guests enjoying their ice cream cake. Maybe the haunted stillness of an empty downstairs.

His foot aches. The wind chimes by the mess hall ring sweetly in the breeze. There is a rusty stain the size of a quarter near the knuckles of his toes. Beneath his heel, his footprints walk backwards in the dust towards the outhouse, crossing the tracks of the last stragglers to leave the compound the day before. He hadn't seen what color the snake had been. He hadn't even heard its rattle. He'd been lost in thought, in a fog, like he is now, considering absently the list of supplies his group had taken with them when they left. The water filter. The cigarettes. The medical kit.

There is a pencil in his hand. He is having a hard time keeping it between his fingers, and the air has become thick, like pillows against his skin, pressing him into a stupor. The wind chimes sing with watery laughter. He tastes a film on his lips, sweet like the sage on the wind, like sugar and chocolate. His hand is moving, he can feel the pressure of the pencil on the notepad. The graphite scrapes in loops, ripping a little black wound into the edge of the paper, and now he is talking, or at least his lips are moving, the air pulling and pushing between them voicelessly, willing his hand to move in shapes he knows, saying *thank you, thank you, thank you all so much for coming.*

Weekday Jesus

Weekday Jesus gets off at 5:00, about an hour after the afternoon crucifixion is over. In the locker room he takes a shower and stows his blood-stained tunic in a mesh gym bag that hangs from a hook on the wall. Someone has left up a string of white Christmas lights along the frame of the locker room door—the kind made for outdoor environments, for tall oak trees and restaurant patios, strung inside a long tube of clear plastic. They were there when Weekday Jesus first started the job. An inheritance from the previous Weekday Jesus.

He rolls on deodorant and sits on the bench, methodically tying the knots on his Chuck Taylors until the bows are even on each side. He has become invested in this recently, having those bows match. Each time he works on the laces, he starts adding new rules. He counts when he ties, 20 seconds or less. No pulling after the initial tie—if they don't match, he starts over. It has become the longest part of his ritual, the punctuation at the end of a sentence he repeats Monday through Friday, 11:00 to 5:00, beginning and ending with the same plea to the Father who never, ever listens.

He sometimes runs into Weekend Jesus at the Ralph's off of Santa Monica. Weekend Jesus has a real beard, groomed intentionally to look unintentional. Weekend Jesus wears tight fitting T-shirts with the logos of softball teams on them, tucked into pressed khakis that stop too high above his ankles. He is there today, absently walking up and down the salad bar, pretending to choose a dressing while a woman with sandy hair and a tank top leans in to use the tongs. Weekday Jesus skips the salad bar.

His father had been a kale farmer in rural Maryland, working on land they'd bought from another farmer who'd bred racing dogs. There was even a barn, which Weekday Jesus' family had used to park his father's collection of period cars, each with its own malady, each assembled in some state of incompleteness. A '68 Corvette, the first of the restyles, without tires and propped in a corner on blocks. A '75 Firebird, missing its 7.5 liter V8. A vivisected MG that his father tried rebuilding from scratch, its guts neatly separated and displayed on wooden tables amidst a graveyard of oil cans. There'd been moments of curiosity which lead to belt marks on Weekday Jesus' legs and buttocks. His father's cars were private things.

When he's checking out, he sees Weekend Jesus helping the sandy-haired woman load her groceries onto the checkout counter. The clerk has this fantastic look, a portrait of the purely unimpressed, but Weekend Jesus is working with his hands, talking in soft tones with a smile that flashes white enough to recompose his face, to cast that beard as a charming maneuver of fashion. The woman is smiling too, her smile more coffee-colored, but Weekend Jesus is not put off by this. There is a joke about salad and they both laugh. Then they are silhouettes in the doorway, enveloped in the white heat of the parking lot and gone, and Weekday Jesus gives the clerk his Ralph's card. Tomorrow is Saturday, he thinks. Time for somebody else to do all the apologizing.

Shackleton's Homecoming

There is no context for the ground in this way, no crow's nest or mountain peak high enough to deliver to Shackleton the picture that is now scrolling by outside the starboard window. The pilot sitting next to him points to the altimeter and smiles. The pilot has a face that defies an easy guess at his age. Clear, coal-fired eyes, angular lines all smoothed out in aftershave. He has a ruddy flush running down the skin of his neck to the white-pressed collar of his uniform. The Air Force Lieutenant back at Tierra del Fuego had told Shackleton that his pilot was a vet of both wars. He'd flown scout planes with canvas wings, lead a squadron in the Battle of Britain, even been a part of the firebombing of German industry following Hitler's retreat into the Rhineland. It was as if he'd been born and raised in the air, Shackleton thinks. A life in the belly of this machine, gifted the pulse of four engines like mechanical hearts, systems to keep the body going in the white emptiness that now spreads out beneath them.

"You know, we were sure the war would be over when our men were rescued," Shackleton says, raising his voice to match the roar of the propellers. The pilot nods slightly in his direction, eyes locked forward as the plane passes through a cloud-break. Below and ahead, beneath a crescent of deep blue, a brilliant stretch of ice unfolds to the horizon. Shackleton gasps. Shackleton leans forward in the copilot's seat, his breath fogging the windows.

"Can we go lower?" he shouts.

The B-29 dips its wing and begins a long, slow turn, low enough now for the sunlight reflecting off the ice to dance along the ceiling of the cockpit in glowing waves. Shackleton's nose is numb, the tips of his beard kissed with frost as he scans the cliffs and bays and ice-cut fjords. He turns away only to check their coordinates, and to glance at the yellowed pages of a journal with a twice-wrapped leather cover, the material crisscrossed with fine webs of age. The pilot watches him, seems to recognize the disturbed look on Shackleton's face. He clears his throat. "I wanted to tell you," he shouts as he pulls the throttle back and steepens the bank of the plane, "that the first flight I ever made over enemy lines was at the Somme."

Shackleton's eyes stay fixed on the ice below.

"I actually worked the bomb sight in the second war," the pilot continues, "but in the Great War they had trouble finding anybody crazy enough to get into the cockpit of a plane. I volunteered because I was too afraid to fire a gun. It seemed the cowardly choice to me at the time."

Shackleton is half-listening. He pictures the faces of his men in the longboat, making ready to leave camp and strike out for civilization. He remembers talking with Tom Crean by the light of penguin blubber lamps, drawing up the plans for their great escape. On Crean's face, as upon the faces of all the men, he'd seen the consciousness of the debate they were having, the indecision over whether to stay on the ice or get in the boats, over which choice was foolish and which was smart, which brave, which weak.

"When I came out below the clouds," the pilot shouts, "nothing looked familiar at all. I'd known the French countryside as a boy. My father had studied in France and we'd spent summers at a farmstead in Moncheaux. But this time, from the plane, it was like no world I'd ever known. The trees were gone. The grass was gone. The only smoke came from the trench lines. Everywhere else there was nothing left to burn."

Below the plane, the ice in the Weddell Sea buckles and cracks, a white skin that hums underneath with a disquiet that Shackleton can still feel 30 years later. He wonders if he really expected to recognize his expedition's camp somewhere down there. In his dreams he had imagined seeing some piece of the *Endurance* washed up on an ice floe—a piece of the mizzen mast or maybe a chunk of mahogany from the wheel house. But now that he's up this high, he realizes that he hadn't been able to picture what the world looks like from the air, this patchwork quilt of miniature sameness. And now beneath him is a shifting glacier that erodes and refreezes each year, that calves in great cataclysms and sends waves rushing along the coast. Waves that scour the shore clean, cold and new again, day after day.

"I flew blind in the smoke from those trenches for hours," the pilot says, banking once more until the Antarctic continent slides past their windows and the great southern ocean opens up ahead. "When I was flying on empty I looked out and somehow found myself at the English Channel. I'd never been happier to see the coast in my life."

Shackleton nods. He touches the inside of the hull of the cockpit, feeling the vibration of the engines on the surface and the rush of the air just outside. He closes his eyes, sensing the drop beyond the metal, the wind so cold it freezes his eyes shut, the water that closes so darkly along the hull of his tiny boat, pulling him out and away into the void. Gently, reverently, he stows away his journal and opens his eyes back to the ocean.

Dream of the Cosmonaut

Laika fell to Earth in a small metallic bubble, a 10-minute free fall that glowed white in the morning sky. Her parachute cords caught in an acacia tree and her capsule popped open on a timer, the inner cockpit catapulting free through a skin of coiled steam. When she opened her eyes, she saw a deep wheel of blue and the faint trace of the moon above her, already washed thin by the sunrise. She found her legs underneath her and licked the dew from the grass. Behind her, the acacia tree caught fire. The farmer found her this way, framed against the fire, sitting patiently and tasting the air.

The farmer's sons had died in war. Silence and the Texas wind occupied the rooms of his house. At first, he would wake up in a panic at night to the *click click click* of Laika's paws along the hardwood hallway. He'd forget, say his sons' names, staring into the darkness at the shape that bobbed in the doorway. Laika would settle onto the floor and give a heavy sigh, like the rush of water in the downstairs pipes when someone turned on the shower. Then the farmer would close his eyes, listening to the dog's rhythmic puffs of breath, a faint, steady engine that never got further away.

When Neil Armstrong walked on the moon, the farmer cut the front page from the Daily Sentinel and pinned it to the cupboard above her water bowl. He stirred his coffee with a butter knife and eyed Laika from the breakfast table. Sunlight cut across the peeled linoleum floor and caught in her fur like golden water. He stroked her along the ruff of her jawline. *Did you see this, dog?* He asked. *Did you make it this far?*

The farmer buried her by the husk of the acacia tree, the grave cradled by the shadow of its limbs at sunset. He wrapped the newspaper clipping and a plastic Loch Ness monster from his sons' toy chest in a blanket with the body. The burnt scraps of metal from her escape pod he kept hidden in the tractor shed, beneath a rusted stack of sheet metal roofing. Children of the subsequent owners of the farm eventually found the escape pod during a game of hide and seek. There were two of them, both boys. They looked at the hammer and sickle on the inside of the heat shield, sucking their teeth and eyeing the driveway where their father's truck was parked. They decided to make the shed a base of operations for the villains of their games. A prison for downed pilots. The KGB secret command. Lex Luthor's kryptonite mine. Afterwards, when the moon began to press through the yellow haze of evening, they would sit beneath the acacia tree and observe their battlefield, scratching epitaphs in the dirt until a call for dinner pulled them home.

The Refold

When the Buick ahead of him swerved off the road, there was a moment when Oliver could see the backseat passenger's hair levitate, as if she'd been shuffling in sockfeet across a shag carpet. Her hand drifted to the ceiling, and then the car was suddenly perpendicular to the highway, rolling forward and upward, the morning sun exploding in a camera flash across the burgundy paint job. Oliver hit the brakes so hard his foot slipped off the pedal. His truck lurched, and he felt a sickening drift to the right, then the left, then finally a resettling back between the lines, the Buick now gone and the pavement ahead of him unspooling empty and white. For a few seconds he drove on. He listened to the hum of the engine, the southern twang of Randy White pitching chew on the radio, the muffled pulses of his breath that sounded staticky, like a microphone with the gain all the way up. Finally, he turned the wheel and let his truck idle to a stop on the shoulder of the highway.

The Buick was about 200 yards back, upside down at the bottom of a ditch to the left of the road. It had shaved a path through a stand of sapling pines, most of which were now folded and pressed beneath the roof. Oliver was surprised to see that his truck was the only vehicle pulled over. He wondered if he was the only one to see the crash. He looked down from the road's edge, feeling the air vibrate with passing traffic, wiping his palms on his jeans, saying *OK, OK, OK* out loud before taking the slope in baby steps, approaching the Buick like it was a wounded animal.

*

I can't believe nobody else stopped, the Human Resources lady he is sleeping with will say later that night, the eee sound of *believe* stretched out in a teenager-y way that Oliver feels is both demeaning and sort of attractive. She'll curl her toes against his and ask him what happened next, and he'll continue, wondering why the details are already hard to put into order, why he can't even remember where along I-59 the accident happened. He'll remember the heat of the pavement. The musk of bluestem shaved back from the shoulder. A bright dome of sky webbed with contrails. He'll remember trying to keep his voice under control when he called 911, but in a way that made him sound bubbly, almost happy, and he'll wonder if he actually was happy right then, standing on the edge of the highway, feeling his body hum with the sensation of being so close to violence, so profoundly and inarguably alive.

*

The only words he consciously spoke were "turn off the car." These were to the driver, who, for a painfully long stretch of time, Oliver thought might be dead. The driver was an older guy, dressed in grey slacks and a short-sleeve yellow work shirt that was pebbled in the creases with broken glass. He was lying on the ceiling with his feet out the window, his torso tangled in his seatbelt. Gasoline vapors shimmered and bent the sunlight around him. Oliver will tell the Human Resources lady that he reached into the car and turned the keys himself, but he didn't. He meant to. His words meant for this action to happen, but after a few seconds with the engine ticking and the wheels spinning freely in the air, the old man groaned and reached for the ignition.

*

Because she'll ask, Oliver will tell the Human Resources lady that the first thing rescue crews did when they arrived was spray the smoking underbelly of the car with white foam. They cut the woman in the back seat out with a pair of oversized hydraulic scissors, and when she emerged, she too was soaked with foam. The Human Resources lady will giggle at this detail, but her face will quickly turn solemn again, sensing Oliver's seriousness and not meaning to offend him. He'll look out the motel window at the bugs circling a streetlamp in the parking lot. Then, without considering why he's doing it, he'll tell her about something he's never told his wife, about a summer from his youth when a new boy in the neighborhood burned to death in a house fire. The Human Resources lady will make a sound, just vowels, then just breathing. The tangerine glow of the streetlamp will shine on their bare skin. She'll let her hand drift to his shoulder and hold it, and for the rest of the night they'll stay quiet, each of them pretending to sleep while bug-shadows dance along the white spackled ceiling.

*

"We were going to a casino," the old man kept saying to the paramedic, his body rocking in a kind of rhythm. "A casino. A casino. A casino."

*

When he was young, Oliver ran the street games with the neighborhood kids—hide and seek, bicycle races, sometimes dodgeball, which he preferred when he hit puberty because it felt like a type of fighting that the parents who slow-sipped Budweisers on their stoops were willing to condone. The summer of his 14th birthday, a father and son moved into the corner house two numbers down from his. It was a small, white-wood camelback with a sloping front porch and wrought iron bars over windows that reflected sun-squares across the yard in the late afternoon. The father wore suits to work every day, even in the dead-dog heat of New Orleans summer. The son was a ghost and a rumor, a face that only appeared in the window for the first few months. Like most of the neighborhood kids, Oliver wasn't sure a boy even lived in the house until he stumbled upon him in the side garden while chasing buck moths with a tennis racquet one evening. The boy's name was Jeremiah. He was tall and his skin was absurdly pale. He had a perfectly smooth face, doll features, and watery brown eyes that focused just below Oliver's nose when he looked at him.

"Why are you killing those moths with your racquet?" The boy had asked.

Oliver frowned at the question. "Where are you from?"

"Rhode Island," said the boy. His fingers played imaginary piano keys on the tops of his knees. "My mom still lives there."

Oliver couldn't picture Rhode Island on a map, but he imagined a snow-cloaked city of housebound children, all of them clean and pale, all of them flinching when they passed him in the halls.

"These moths lay eggs," he said in his best adult voice, "and in the spring they turn into stinging caterpillars. The more oak tress y'all have in your yard, the more caterpillars y'all'll get."

The boy looked around the canopy of leaves above him, then at the tennis racquet in Oliver's hand. The strings were clotted with orange, pulpy gore. He grinned.

Though he never told anybody about meeting Jeremiah that day, Oliver has since allowed the pages of his memory to refold themselves into a story more fit for telling—that they made friends that evening, that he let the boy have his racquet, that they sat together on the porch until the light was blue and thick with hissing crickets, swinging at shapes in the air until the moon lifted out of the clouds.

*

Over breakfast at Stuckey's, Oliver stirs his grits into his eggs moodily. The Human Resources lady doesn't needle him for small-talk, nor does she tease his leg under the table in the way that makes his breath quicken and his heart feel sore. She seems preoccupied too, and when they're together by the cars, once again at their usual point of departure, she holds his body against hers in a way that normally would make him conscious of who might be watching. *I'm proud of you*, she says. Oliver smiles and feels an odd untangling in his chest.

He recognizes this moment in the way he'd envisioned it yesterday during the adrenal afterglow of the accident, the music pumping in the cab of his truck and his voice lost against the rush of highway air—this realignment of the world and the new paths it offered. Here is where he would tell her that he's quitting the company. Here is where he'd tell her he hates the long commutes, careful not to imply that he hates their affair so much as to show the cumulative strain of it all, to spread around the responsibility for his waning interest. He'd say that the experience with the car crash has led him to reevaluate his life, though maybe he wouldn't say it that way. Maybe he'd stress the visceral thrill of doing good things as a frame for change, smoothing over the details so that it feels convincing to an audience beyond himself. He would choose all the right words, and her belief in the nobility of this idea would be enough to distill it into a solid thing, something he now would feel as surely as the ground pressing upward beneath his feet.

Oliver tallies these thoughts as she swings her denimed hips into the driver's seat of her Toyota. She revs the engine playfully at him, then slowly merges into southbound traffic. He stands in the parking lot for a little while after she's gone, still feeling like the moment hasn't quite finished, a list of rendezvous dates on a napkin in his back pocket, his wedding band snugly in the groove above his knuckle, the sharp smell of burning leaves drifting in like a fogbank from across the access road.

The Confession of Clementine

Clementine didn't understand what upset some people about having Hollywood in town. The production crews weren't pushy, they cleaned up after themselves, and even the equipment guys and rig drivers had been plenty decent around town at night. Locals would crowd about and gawk during shooting, enough so that parish police had to call in state troopers to help keep the peace, but everyone seemed happy enough. She'd overheard Becky Randazzo gush to the Honduran ladies who worked at the Hair 'N' Nails about seeing actors she'd recognized, *in person*, each of them more real for being different than Becky Randazzo had pictured, each of them aglow in ways that Becky Randazzo sternly attributed to late-night-television creams and to the more mystical and apocryphal remedies that she was sure the coastal elite cultivated in their medicine chests. The Honduran ladies clucked and nodded, hands busy, eyes sideways on each other.

Personally, Clementine felt the actors hadn't looked aglow at all. The leading man looked haggard to her, far too pale to play anyone who worked outdoors in Louisiana. She'd first seen him Monday morning, exiting the makeup trailer where it had been set up on old Main, facing the two-block front of brickwork buildings from the original town center, their abandoned storefronts now cleaned to a shine, the mortar re-painted, logos of fake antique stores and mom & pop groceries stenciled along their windows. He smoked the wrong way, she thought. He held the cigarette butt between his thumb and forefinger like he was holding a shoelace, and the dark stubble that crept down his neck contrasted sharply with his smooth, shiny chest. His posture reminded her of an adolescent reluctantly waiting for the school bus, bent by burdens both real and imagined.

Word had spread around town that he was playing a man who kills his family. The movie folks had tried to keep a tight lid on the details of the script, but they hired too many locals to do laundry and meals and big-rig repair for anything to stay a secret for long. When Clementine had caught the leading man standing alone in the shade of the makeup trailer, she'd pulled her station wagon up the hill into the lot of the abandoned Phillips 66 and watched him for a while.

Even though it was barely 9:30, the day's heat piled relentlessly onto the town. It collected in valleys like fog, so that the parking lot she was idling in stood just above a shimmering blanket of humidity, thick enough to make a dog retch. Wind from the southeast drifted through her open windows, mixing the scent of cooked upholstery with a warm odor of pine. Clementine unwrapped a stick of gum, rolled it between her fingers before chewing it, and watched. *A man who kills his family*, she thought. She watched his fingers pinch the cigarette, watched the smoke coiling out as his lips moved. She imagined he was practicing lines, and she tried to conjure the goodbye witticisms of Charles Bronson and Keith Carradine, yet all she heard in her mind was *I'm sorry, my love, I'm so so sorry.*

*

She hadn't meant to kill Randall. She hadn't helped him either, once he'd landed awkwardly between the basement steps and the water heater, but she'd pushed him out of frustration for the way he moved, like a slow drip of honey that never quite got where it was going, and hadn't meant anything beyond an exclamation point that might inject some urgency. Her husband hadn't been looking, though. He had already turned around and opened the basement door, and her eyes had been closed because she always closed her eyes when she searched herself for something truly vile to say to him. He'd been living for months in a kind of sleepwalk state, and that day Clementine had simply had enough of it. In her view, things had gotten worse and worse, her husband solidifying into a statute on the back porch, a corpse on the couch after dinner that communicated with movements so slow and subtle they required time-lapse photography to decipher. Becky Randazzo had jokingly called him *Ran-Dull*, and although she'd never objected to his plain demeanor, Clementine knew that most folks thought she'd married down. Randall was a man destined to go nowhere fast. Randall was large. Randall was kind, though in a disaffected way that best showed itself when he was able to fix your washing machine hose or replace the ballcock in a leaky toilet. And now, on an evening in which all she'd wanted was a bath with enough hot water to soak in, he was lying in the shape of the letter S, his neck at a strange angle against the water heater pipe, his legs still on the steps, curling and straightening involuntarily, little swishes of denim accompanied by the gurgle of his breathing.

Clementine took a few steps down into the basement and stopped where his boots still twitched. Spit bubbles blossomed at Randall's lips, and his large brown eyes were wide and unfocused. There had initially been a sound in her head when he'd fallen, like a scream or a timing belt squealing, but as she crouched there on the steps, she felt it soften into a moan, and then into nothing, until the only sound in the basement was the spit bubbles popping, and then that stopped, too. She was sorry. She was terribly, terribly sorry, and she wanted to say it, but without the bubble sound, the basement was truly silent, and she felt that words might somehow upset the calm that had closed in around them. She'd always hated the way her voice sounded when she'd scolded him in the past, the way they'd broken his little worlds of quiet. She didn't resent him for taking the buyout from Gaylord Chemical after the accident, but she still came to dread finding him sitting on the back porch each time she came home from running errands. She didn't even resent that he'd taken to smoking reefer with his cousin, a worthless rag-and-bone guy from Picayune who started growing fields of the stuff in the Homochitto National Forest once budget cutbacks got all the park rangers laid off.

What she did resent, as far as she could understand it, was that the new normal—the both of them in his family's ancestral home, together each day and night without punctuation unless she took it upon herself to go out—revealed the truth in that silly distinction between simply loving someone and being in love with them. It was the kind of thing she imagined the unfairly pretty girls from high school would have debated about their boyfriends. But silly or not, this distinction had filled in the quiet spaces between Randall and herself. It had widened the bed between their bodies at night and left them suspended in a comfortable but coldly perfunctory sense of each other's presence in the house.

And so, after the initial shock faded, and after several minutes of silence on the steps, she found herself considering, without any conscious effort to do so, the bottom of her husband's boots. *Were they wet?* she wondered. Had he, perhaps, slipped? Had she come home from shopping to find him dead and then fallen to pieces right there on the steps, too out-of-sorts to think to call the authorities until it was too late? How long would it take to get everything settled? Would the ladies who ran the hearts game gossip, would that bitch Becky Randazzo say she'd done it for the money? Would a court let her inherit her husband's house, indeed, his benefit checks, in the case of a suspicious accident?

She sat for a long time and thought, crouched on the dark stairwell until her knees ached, feeling the cool basement stillness on her skin like she was submerged in a swimming pool, her breath in shallow beats that barely seemed to move the air at all.

*

"Mrs. Randall Grandbouche?" the man at the door asked. Clementine winced at the use of her husband's name, her eyes adjusting to the morning sunlight that baked the east-facing entrance of her home through a gap in the pines. Sweet olive blossoms skipped across the porch in the breeze.

"If you're from the witnesses I already told them we're members of Westside Emmanuel Baptist," she said.

The man in the doorway was angular, dressed in a tight-fitting suit and skinny tie, sweating heavily so that his dark skin glistened and stained his collar. His hair was piled into a kind of shark's fin that ran down the middle of his skull, the sides of his scalp shaved smooth and his teeth an almost chemical shade of white.

"Ma'am, my name is Eduardo Fragoza," he said, holding up a stack of manila folders from under his arm as if they helped explain what this meant. Behind him, she noticed a white SUV idling in the drive, several other men in suits visible through the windows, all of them in dark sunglasses. Eduardo looked over her shoulder into the house, then back to Clementine. "By any chance is your husband home?"

Clementine felt her breakfast shifting in her stomach. She wanted to shut the door softly, hoping that by not slamming it she wouldn't seem overly rude, but instead she found herself searching for a badge on the man's suit. He was well-dressed, perhaps overly so for any Washington Parish deputy. Eduardo had a manila folder open in his hands. He was looking back at the SUV, where another young man had stepped out the passenger side but now stopped and watched them both. The man at the car pulled out a cigarette and Eduardo broke the silence with an awkward laugh. "Perhaps," he said, "Randall is at work somewhere that we might reach him?"

"I'm afraid not," She said, without offering more.

"Are you a decision-maker of the household?" Eduardo asked. She paused, certain now at least that Eduardo and his crew were not, in fact, with the sheriff's office.

"Decision-maker in what way?" she asked.

Eduardo motioned up at the eaves of her porch, to the tall French windows overlooking the magnolias in the side yard. "Decision-maker as in, can you make important decisions about your property," he said.

"Like, selling it?"

"Not selling, no," Eduardo said, flipping through glossy photos in his folder. She saw real estate listings, big color spreads of southern mansions and plantations. Curious, she leaned in.

"That's the Fontainebleau place up by the river," she said, pointing to a photo.

"Mrs. Grandbouche, I'm an assistant producer for the project being shot in parts of Bogalusa." Eduardo scanned across her windows as he spoke to her. "I'm not sure if you were aware that we were making a movie in town, but we've been looking at houses in the area—truly, all up and down the Mississippi—that might fit a certain style our director is looking for."

Clementine felt a sudden compulsion for a cigarette. Freight cars rumbled across Coburn Creek in the distance. She pictured the leading man, down on Main in the shade of that trailer. She saw him turn his head as he inhaled white smoke, handing his zippo to her with a smile, laughing about the heat while they sat on folding chairs. Behind Eduardo, the SUV honked its horn.

"Mrs. Grandbouche, how do you feel about horror movies?" Eduardo asked.

*

Her first plan involved a river. The Mississippi was the better option; its bed had been dredged deep and its undertow drowned plenty of folks each year. Randall had no business over by the Mississippi though, and driving his body 50 miles west to Baton Rouge seemed like a wild risk. The Pearl was close by, and if he floated the short distance down to the Bogue Chitto Wildlife Refuge he might disappear. But anglers and trappers still used the refuge, and this stretch of the Pearl was shallow. It wound around broad sandbar points, and its banks were choked with treefall that could easily snag a corpse. Both rivers were dangerous, but she certainly had to do something. The bugs would be on him by morning, and she knew that he'd start to stink soon, even in the cool air of the basement.

What Clementine had not accounted for was the weight of the dead. She'd gathered a bed sheet and a spare shower curtain from the closet, laid each out on the unfinished dirt floor of the basement, then slowly rolled Randall across them, winding his head and feet with duct tape until all of him was hidden from view. When she tried to lift him, however, Randall simply slipped out of her hands and slid to the bottom of the steps. She would bend at the knees, heave until she saw stars, and the process would repeat itself. It was as if Randall's corpse was stone, had always been stone, and in its permanent stillness had finally gained the gravity that pulled on him so heavily in life. Clementine knelt by Randall and wept until she was empty. There would be no arguing it.

She left the body and went upstairs to draw a bath. The water was tepid, and she sat still and drank blackberry wine until it layered a syrupy film along her tongue and her skin became gooseflesh. Strange, apocalyptic visions danced in the candlelight by the tub. She saw her house in flames, firemen holding her by the shoulders while she screamed her husband's name. She saw a greasy orange plume mushroom up into a blue morning sky, followed by a rain that melted the town to its foundations. Then she saw her father standing in a black and shining river, the water like glass as he dipped his head beneath the surface and stood again, his clothes stripped free and spiraling downstream into darkness.

*

Whatever doubts had lingered with Clementine through the week were eased by Becky Randazzo's reaction. To be fair, Becky Randazzo had barely reacted at all, but Clementine was already basking in the echo of this absence, this deliciously false calm that Becky now exhibited as she collected the cards and helped Dianne carry wine glasses to the rec room. She'd waited the whole game of hearts to mention anything about the movie, to talk about Eduardo and his fellow suits, about the twin doublewides now parked along the west lawn of her property, about the porta-potties they were polite enough to bring in so that the crew wasn't constantly using her toilet. It was like secretly holding a winning hand, Clementine thought, a bubbling thrill that allowed the surreal horror with Randall to fade mercifully into the ether.

A few minutes earlier, as the game was winding down, Becky had brought up the settlement negotiations with Gaylord Chemical—a topic everyone at the table was sick of, but which lingered like a figurative residue all over town. A decade earlier, on a crisp October morning, a train car offloading dinitrogen tetroxide just outside of town had exploded. The sky turned orange for days, forcing parish-wide evacuations and leaving Bogalusa empty until NARAC inspectors grudgingly gave the all-clear. There were strange morning fogs for weeks, and the corpses of stray cats and dogs washed up along Coburn Creek through Christmas. Even years after the accident, visitors would comment on the sour, metallic odor that crept up from the ground on hot summer days. Most of the residents had been part of a group settlement, but Becky's home had been only a few hundred yards from the processing plant and was leveled by the blast. Her lawyers had promised her millions, some of which she already spent on the down-payment for a stone-and-sheetrock mansion behind the country club. The house was only half-built, however, so Becky often complained about having to sleep in the dining room while she waited for the 2nd floor to be finished. And for the money to finish it.

"I use Pine Sol on the floors three times a week," Becky was saying, "and I still get the smell sometimes."

"Anything with ammonia brings it back for me," Diane said, vertical fractures ridging the concealer on her nose as she scowled.

"I'm thinking about re-painting," Becky said. "The LeBlancs said they painted the bedrooms a second time and they can't smell anything now."

"The LeBlancs are creole trash," said Florence, the octogenarian stenographer.

"The smell reminds me of the old Phillips 66," Clementine said, fanning and stacking her cards with precision. "We used to go there in high school, back when there were live oaks by the lot that you could sit behind without anyone seeing you. We'd drink beers under those trees and watch the cars cruise up Sullivan to Sunset. My breath smelled like yeast and my dresses stank of motor oil. That's the closest thing to the smell I can think of."

"Did you ever let Ran-Dull cop a feel there?" Becky asked. Diane giggled. Clementine felt heat bloom on her skin, dissolving an image of a freckled boy whose name she'd forgotten, a beer bottle that had sweated a ring on her knee, the steady *chunk chunk* of the gas pumps counting out the dollars.

"Randall and I hadn't met in high school," Clementine said.

"True love waits," Becky sang. Clementine pictured Randall's eyes in the semi-dark of their basement; curious, marbled over, holding the light from the doorway in a static starburst. She felt the air on her skin again, the pocket of silence she'd kept.

"They're using our house for the movie," she said.

Diane coughed and then made a hooting sound. Becky's smile loosened, then her brow tilted with a look of such genuinely awkward surprise that Clementine wished she'd had the guts to take a picture.

"Shoot the moon!" Florence croaked, laying out her cards.

*

The production was in full-swing, and Clementine passed the days in a stupor of day-drinking and vague optimism until Eduardo found her at the crew lunch table and told her that a priest was going to need to go into the basement. A week earlier, after digging a trench for Randall and buying powdered lime and a couple of bags of quick-mix, she'd put up a note—*Wet Cement*—in heavy black sharpie on the basement door. She'd even locked the door handle (something neither she nor Randall had ever done in their years together) with a key she stashed deep in her purse, but now, after days of exterior shots and an ugly weather forecast, the production was shifting indoors.

"The priest is supposed to be exorcising the house," Eduardo said, uncapping a bottle of water from the catering table on the front lawn. "He's going to say the words, spray the holy water, the whole shebang. He's got to be thorough."

Clementine let the words sink in, chewing on a snickerdoodle and practicing her non-reaction. In the short time she had known him, she'd come to admire Eduardo's composure, and she felt herself mimicking his mannerisms now and then when sudden fits of panic crept up on her. "Does he really have to go into every room?" she asked.

"We have to shoot it," he said, "even if we don't use it."

She stared at the hummus-boat that sailed upon a sea of stale pita triangles. Crew members shuffled around, munching finger sandwiches and checking their smartphones. She imagined what her minister would say about a Catholic exorcism—even a fake one—in her house.

"You honestly wouldn't believe how much footage we don't use," Eduardo said, stretching his back and then patting her shoulders apologetically. "When my uncle was in the business the ratio used to be 5:1, film-to-final cut. Nowadays you've got crane shots, POV shots, Go-Pros on your ceiling fans; it's bananas. We could make a kids' movie, a romance, and a murder mystery by the time this is over."

"What if the cement isn't dry?" Clementine asked, "Can't you just shoot the basement scene in a studio or something?"

Eduardo tossed his water bottle into a recycling bin and checked his watch. "I'll talk to Dave about it," he said, "but you should look over the contract again and see if you can find a way to let them have what they want." He motioned with his hand around the yard, eyeing the charcoal clouds boiling up from the south. "Problems make themselves; we don't need to add to the pile."

*

Clementine sat on the sloping lawn for the remainder of the afternoon, cookies crumbling in the pockets of her jeans, the grass warm under her rump. The whine of vacuum cleaners and the hiss of pressure washers drifted in the wet air. Crew members moved in a steady line from her front door to a U-Haul parked at the end of the lane, carrying out the individually bubble-wrapped pieces of her life with Randall in ones and twos. Another truck with rental furniture waited by the mailboxes down the road. Clementine's head throbbed. Thoughts of the camera crew in her basement had tightened her stomach into a hard pit. The concrete should have set by now, but she didn't know for sure. She flicked ants from her toes and wondered how her house must look to other people now, with its guts spilled out and its bones being scrubbed and polished. What kind of home would the crew build inside? There would probably be boutique-y accents everywhere, mason-jar candles and pressed-tin backsplash, the kind of tacky shit Becky Randazzo would earmark in Skymall, and Clementine suddenly felt a heaviness in her body that she knew was much deeper than simple sorrow. There was portent in all of this. Hollywood was going to murder a fictional family on rented furniture somewhere in her home, as if they'd seen it through the magnolia trees from a distance and known everything she'd hidden underneath. She wondered what these strangers saw in Bogalusa—what they really saw in the pecan-shaded yards, the trailers hidden beyond longleaf pine, the crumbling cemeteries and the formaldehyde grandeur of the plantations along the river.

Below her, a man—a local, she guessed, by the camo rain pants and the faded cap pulled low over greasy brown curls—came walking up the drive from the road, his hands thrust deep in his pockets. He had a backpack slung over one boney shoulder, and Clementine sensed something familiar in his posture. She watched him approach the crewmen loading her furniture, then slip behind the truck. Through the truck's windows she saw the local laugh, then turn around, backpack-less, a cigarette between his lips as he walked back down the drive. He paused to fiddle with a lighter, and then Clementine felt her lungs deflate as she recognized who it was. Randall's worthless cousin grinned, exhaling a white trail of smoke, a wad of twenties folded in his skeletal hand as he tipped the brim of his hat in her direction.

*

The rain finally quit Saturday afternoon. Clementine lounged on the slippery plastic recliner by her hotel pool, watching Randall's cousin sink himself to the bottom and resurface over and over again. The sun baked the concrete dry, and Clementine held the reefer deep in her lungs, feeling alternating tides of calm and panic swell across her body. The cousin's torso was bright white, scripted with blue graffiti across his midriff and acne-scarred shoulders. His curly hair was slicked back while he rotated in a circle.

"I'm a sprinkler," he said, spitting widgets of pool water in lazy arcs.

She had planned to call the cops on him. She was going to do it today, but she hadn't worked out all the details, and now that she was high and warm and flecked with mist from the pool she felt the urgency of things diminishing. He'd been curious about her husband, and skeptical that Randall might have travelled up to the Homochitto alone without calling. *He doesn't talk to me anymore about anything*, Clementine had said. *When he left I assumed he'd gone to see you*, but Randall's cousin just gave her a dead-eyed look and shook his head. *He ain't been up my way since the fourth of July*, he'd said.

She hadn't asked how Randall's cousin had come to supply the movie crew with pot, but she knew his presence was a threat in more ways than she could calculate. Each step seemed fraught, like stepping further into a pond without knowing how deep it really went. She didn't want trouble for the movie, but she couldn't have the cousin asking questions until she'd devised a better story for what happened to Randall.

In the out-loud voice of her thinking, the plan was to get him locked up for possession for a while, anonymously, just to get him out of the way. The cousin wasn't a bad guy, really. Except for his stature, he was actually a lot like Randall. It was a humane means to an end, Clementine had concluded, and useful leverage against his credibility if he raised suspicions about Randall's disappearance later on. She would listen to this out-loud voice make its case, but when she closed her eyes she would picture a different scene, snapshots from a plot where the evidence leads back to the Homochitto, and from there to different stories about a missing man and a pot farm and a hungry wilderness that swallowed the dead and kept them.

Clementine glanced westward, through the chain link fence towards her neighborhood, and wondered what Eduardo was doing with the house. She inhaled and imagined that somewhere beyond Randall's family home up on the hill there was another house on the coast, nothing too modern, something with a modest view. There would be a salt tang on the breeze, a shopping trip into town, a blithe consideration of what to do and who to be next. *What safety in acting*, she thought, and her chest began to ache.

"Watch me," the cousin cooed, scissor-kicking imaginary enemies in slow motion beneath the sparkling surface.

*

The temperature on the final day of production was 88 degrees at sunrise. The camera crew sweated and cursed. Gaffers tucked bottles of ice water down their pants. The priest sat in a swivel chair and drank a tallboy of Bud Light in the shade of the makeup trailer where, after a lengthy delay, the leading man emerged. He had grown his stubble out into something approaching a real beard, though it was patchy and unkempt, authentic to the day laborers and laid-off railroad men Clementine sometimes saw gathered at dawn in the parking lot of the Home Depot. "This is to show the passage of time," Eduardo had explained earlier, "and to show that he's going crazy."

The leading man was shirtless, and someone had ladled lines of red food coloring across his chest and forearms in a splatter pattern. His hair looked unwashed, and his eyes were painted into hollow recesses by heavy mascara. Eduardo shouted *Ten minutes!* The priest burped, tossed his beer can, and got up to join the crew assembling on the porch. The leading man sat down and closed his eyes. The yard slowly emptied, and a close and familiar quiet descended into the magnolia shade as Clementine cautiously stepped forward.

"Do you like the house?" she asked in a tiny voice.

The leading man blinked at the hunched woman who had materialized next to him, her arms folded as if she were cold. He let out a long sigh but said nothing.

"Is it like your own house?" Clementine said again, opening a pack of cigarettes and offering him one. "I bet it isn't, but I don't know what California houses look like."

The leading man glanced up at the meeting on the porch. There, Eduardo was coaching up the priest, thrusting a plastic crucifix forward energetically, casting out the demons.

"I'm from New Mexico," he said softly. He took a cigarette and nodded.

"I figured people in movies lived in mansions in Los Angeles," Clementine said, "or maybe in Malibu in those beach bungalows on stilts by the water."

"Living there doesn't make you from there," the man said.

Clementine startled herself with a laugh, a little peep like a bird call or a hiccup, and she knelt down on the lawn next to him.

"Most folks here are from here, I suppose," she said. "This house was in my husband's family for generations, back to when it was part of a pecan farm." She felt the pause that followed, and in it a welling up of different words, a jumble of stories that suddenly flooded over her all at once. She wanted to tell him all the negligible little nothings that had dislodged themselves in her mind, the snipes from Becky Randazzo and the tyranny of little dreams that had closed in over everyone she knew in Bogalusa and kept them sleepwalking there. Seconds crawled by, syllables starting and dying on her lips one by one until she feared the conversation had ended just when she understood now how much she needed it to continue.

"My dad wanted to be a farmer," the leading man said.

"Can you farm in New Mexico?"

"Some places maybe. But not in Truth or Consequences."

"That's a dramatic name," Clementine said.

He smiled ruefully. "It used to just be called Hot Springs," he said. "They changed it for a radio show. Not all that dramatic."

"It sounds biblical," Clementine said, scanning anvil-shaped clouds that towered up in white columns to the west. "What does it mean?"

"It used to mean there were hot springs nearby I guess. I never heard the radio show."

"I read in high school that Bogalusa means *dark water* in Choctaw," Clementine said. She was surprised she'd said this, but saying it brought to mind a kaleidoscope of images she hadn't pictured in years. She remembered the coffee-brown creeks and sandbars of her youth, of trash in the trees at the waterline and the bouncing gurgle of submerged logs that her father had called dead men.

"Scary name," he said, grinning. "Good for a movie."

On the front steps, the girl who played the leading man's daughter fiddled with a tablet computer while several makeup artists painted blood and gore onto her neck. The leading man watched her.

"You know, we actually had a serial killer back home," he said. "They caught him when I was away at college. The man and his wife kidnapped women and tortured them in a trailer; did this for twenty years or something before one woman finally escaped."

Clementine was listening, but she felt strangely detached, her mind pulling away from the words the man spoke, a hot air balloon caught in the thermals. The leading man's eyes shone with a sudden, liquid intensity.

"I've never played a murderer before," he continued. "They make me read all this sick stuff to get me ready for the role, but none of it sticks the way it should. I know more facts about serial killers than I ever wanted to, but when I'm supposed to be a killer—you know, like, be inside his mind—they tell me I have to make it personal. They tell me to conjure up all of the most horrible things I've ever felt and hold on to them. The weird disgust I get when I hold people's babies. The horror when I learned my brother got run over by a drunk driver. The urge I used to have, on bad days when I was a kid, to just beat the shit out of my dad with his Ty Cobb replica bat and run away to Canada."

Clementine heard sirens in the distance. She imagined the flashing lights from a thousand feet above, winding through the trees towards the motel where she was sure Randall's cousin was fast asleep. There had been this sense of motion when she'd woken up that morning, something like standing in an elevator and feeling the pressure shift as it climbed. She knew she could not hold all the ends anymore. She could not see where the strings would end up when they unwound, but she'd known, as she watched the dust motes spin in the dawn filtering through the hotel room shades, that the world was now shifting beyond her grasp, beyond the fingertips of Eduardo and Becky Randazzo and the half-drunk priest who was shouting *take hold of the serpent, bind him and cast him into the bottomless pit!* at a light fixture on the porch.

"I don't know if it's possible," the leading man said. "You know, to go there and come back again."

The sirens moaned louder. She look at him, this mirage of a man, soon to fade, shimmering now in her yard. She felt her lips open. She felt her tongue shape the first words and the ones that followed, all the things he would now need to know.

Reclamation

Everyone had a different opinion about where the old man kept the head. Marco's guess was in the freezer, but the rest of us thought that was gross. "It would touch the ice trays," said Ernesto, "and then you'd have rotten head-water in your coke."

"Jeffrey Dahmer kept his heads in the freezer," Marco said, but nobody wanted to argue with Marco about what Jeffery Dahmer did. Nobody stuck up for the idea either. Instead, Fat Travis made a sound with his mouth like shovel scraping on cement, then puffed his cheeks and spat towards the river. The spit caught the wind and did a little pirouette in the air, spreading into a string that draped across the spearpoints of cattails at the base of the levee. The sun baked our stomachs. Super-heated concrete cooked our backs.

"Think how much the head would stink if he didn't keep it cold," Marco said after a while.

Ernesto looked skeptical. "So he's just had it in his freezer for like, 50 years?"

"How else would he keep it from stinking?"

Marco was exhausted by how obvious this all was. Ahead of us, along the upstream curve of the Mississippi, the bow of a tanker swung out into the center channel. Cloud shadows slipped across the boiling water.

"Big one," said Fat Travis.

"Offloaded already," said Ernesto.

"Foreign flag," I said, though I couldn't see nearly that far. The grain tankers were usually foreign, sometimes double or triple-flagged above the wheelhouse, strange colors and patterns rippling in the wind. If someone knew the flag by sight they took the points. Otherwise it was the first person to read the port of registry on the stern when the ship passed.

"Ya'll wouldn't know about the stink because Uptown didn't lose power during the storm," Marco said.

"Like hell we didn't," said Fat Travis.

"How do you know?" Marco asked. "You evacuated."

"All the clocks were flashing when we got back," Travis said. "My dad's chest-freezer had melted and all his deer meat rotted."

"See?" Marco said. "If you think warm deer meat stinks, imagine a human head."

Our house had lost power during Hurricane Andrew too. Our house sometimes lost power on sunny days, and it seemed to me that the grid in New Orleans was always on the verge of falling apart. The black-tar poles on our street were tilted at an angle, their lines sagging between the gnarled branches of live oaks. In some places, loose lengths of wire danced free in the wind.

"If he kept it in the freezer it'd be rotten by now 'cause of the outage," Fat Travis said, "so he probably preserved it another way."

"Like a mummy," Ernesto said.

"Like a mummy," Fat Travis said.

"Ireland," I shouted, "points are mine!"

"The colors are backwards," said Ernesto.

"The fuck do you know," I said.

"I'm Irish."

Ernesto laughed at his own joke, then grinned below the stubble of his early-onset mustache.

"A mummy head would be less cool," Marco said, digging his fingers into the cracks in the levee. A cloud drifted across the spot where we were lying. "It would be all wrinkled and shrink-wrap looking."

I was waiting for the stern of the tanker ship to come into view, but it was taking its time. I thought about how our whole house has smelled like Dad's ham-sandwich farts when we got back after Hurricane Andrew. My mom had opened all the windows, and Dad made an elaborate show of putting grocery bags over his hands while he cleared out the fridge. My brother stopped drinking milk afterwards, said he could taste the smell in his cereal. Dad made his protein shakes with water instead, and those smelled pretty bad too, but my brother drank them for breakfast every morning anyway, and soon after he was twisting my arms and pinching my biceps when we walked to the bus stop.

"A . . . bid . . . jan," Ernesto said, squinting through his glasses at the water, "Côte d'Ivoire."

"That's not English," I said.

"Not Irish either," Ernesto said.

I glared at him, and tried pushing myself to my feet in a single motion, kung-fu style, but the slope of the levee was steeper than it seemed, and my torso rotated too far forward. I staggered down the slope and landed in the muck along the high-water line.

"Bruce Leander," Fat Travis said. The others laughed.

I stood in the grass, feeling the cold creep up my ankles. A cloud of gnats swirled around my head, lit golden in the afternoon sun like the grain dust from the offload towers.

"Fuck all of you," I said. "You're suckers for thinking The Twins wouldn't make that whole story up. You think the old man would just show it off to them for mowing his lawn? Invite them in for lemonade and say, hey, look at this Japanese trophy head I brought back from the war?"

Fat Travis growled up another wad of spit.

"It means Ivory Coast," Ernesto said to nobody in particular. "That's Africa."

I'd had enough. I trudged away up the hill, my shoes squelching with each step, to the ridge where our bikes lay tangled at the edge of the jogging path. Ahead of me, the A-frame attics of Uptown shimmered and melted in the heat. I walked my bike by the handlebars down the city side of the levee, past the anthills to the train tracks that paralleled River Road.

My anger had already left, and embarrassment filled in behind it. Of course I'd only pretended to not-believe. I'd meant to shame them for believing, but the shame was all mine, because I was the sucker who'd bought the story when The Twins first told it. I was the one who'd imagined the scene: a dark parlor that smelled of polished leather, a gaudy wall-display of katana swords in elaborate scabbards, bandoliers of 50-cal ammunition strung about like vines. There would be a glass cube, lit by the kind of track lighting you see in museums, in which would sit a blackened, fleshy thing: a piece of someone that used to be alive, the only piece that could have been alive, empty but not empty, like an abandoned house.

Cars whipped by on River Road. Heat spun up from the blacktop in dusty eddies. I turned back and saw the profile of Ernesto up on the ridge, looking after me, his curly hair flicking in the wind like a black flag.

*

What I wanted and what I got were always different things. What I wanted were D&D books for Christmas from the hobby shop on Airline Drive. What I got were more wool socks than anyone in Louisiana could ever need. What I wanted was to punch my older brother once, suddenly, when he wasn't expecting resistance, and to break his nose so hard that he'd keep his pinching, groping, nipple-twisting hands off of me. What I got was Tai Chi with my mom on Wednesdays, where we memorized a 34-step dance that would put my brother to sleep rather than scare him. What I wanted—what I always wanted—was for my summers to be free. What I got was a multiple-choice exam of non-optional options about camps and around-the-house projects, enforced by nagging and a family-wide discomfort with anything resembling idleness.

I envied The Twins. I would've happily mowed lawns that summer, but the only way for me to get an allowance was to help Dad scrape the old paint off the storm shutters, and this was rough work. July and August were intolerably hot. Thankfully, storms would pop up each afternoon that soaked the city and cut our days short. When the rains came, we scrambled down to the kitchen and watched the streets overfill. While we waited it out, Dad would sometimes crack a High Life and pour some in my orange juice.

Ben got home from wrestling practice right around the time the storms melted away. We wouldn't see him, but we'd hear the crackle of his Walkman and his heavy wet shoes stomping on the stairs. An acrid body-smell followed him from room to room, so sharp it hurt my eyes. It smelled of rubber and salt, like spice and rotting meat. It reminded me of jet fumes, the exhaust of an anger so hot that it fogged the bathroom mirrors.

What my brother wanted and what he got wasn't clear to me. I assumed he wanted sex because he was a senior in high school, because he left crusty hand-towels in the laundry hamper and listened to AC/DC songs about women with well-cleaned motors. What he got were restricted diets, Cs in all his classes, and—at the end of each day—a thorough schooling in more and more complicated ways to hurt people. Pressure points. Arm bars. Pins and escapes. The night he made varsity, he snapped all of my GI Joes at the waist and left their halves in a contorted orgy on the floor.

Most nights my brother wore this slack, half-lidded expression. It was the look of someone who lived somewhere else, who watched a different movie in their mind. I tried not to think about that movie, but when I did, I saw a house in the rain, and inside of it, all of us, bent like dolls, broken into pieces one by one.

*

I spent a lot of my summer imagining casual encounters with Layla, a girl who walked her family's dog around our block. I'd do dry-runs at night, squaring up my skinny-bird shoulders in the shower, puffing my chest with a casual *What's up, Layla* in my deepest, least-warbly voice. Sometimes I stole the best old T-shirts from my dad's drawer to wear while working, just in case she showed.

Layla was a grade below me at Father Son and Holy Ghost Prep. She was mysterious and lovely. Her black hair was luminescent and flat and cut into bangs that were squared across her porcelain brow. She glided around the neighborhood, moving either her arms or her legs but not both at the same time. We'd spoken before in the company—and at the urging—of our parents; *hi*'s and *hey*'s, nothing more, but just being recognized by her felt like an affirmation of something good, like a sudden break in the clouds. The dog she walked was another story. A vibrating, scruffy thing, it had a face that made me think of a mustachioed English gentleman who'd been transformed into a dog by a wizard.

The day after I'd left Ernesto and the group on the levee, I was scraping the front shutters when Layla appeared at the base of the ladder.

"You," she called up to me.

I turned and dropped my putty knife into the garden below.

"Layla," I squeaked, my chest all out of air.

"Leander," she said. "Have you seen my dog?"

"Lee," I said, gripping both rails of the ladder. "No, is he lost?"

"*She* isn't lost, she just got out the screen door after a bath."

I scanned the yard and the alley intently. I willed that little dog to materialize from the bushes, but the air was heavy and still, and nothing at all seemed to be moving.

"I'm sorry," I said, looking like I was going to say more if she stayed around. My breath smelled like yeast.

"It's okay," Layla said, eyeing the alley to our backyard, her arms hanging loose. "Do you need your scraper back?"

"Uh, no," I said, "I'm cool."

She looked at me and the half-stripped shutters skeptically. "You just going to stay up there then?"

"It's nice up here."

"Okay, Lee," she said, putting her hands on her hips and rotating from side to side. "Come by my house if you see her please."

"I will," I said. Then I made a show of scanning the horizon some more until she walked off down Burdette towards St. Charles, stopping occasionally to clap and whistle. Thunderheads towered over the lake to the north. Cicadas began their hiss in the trees. Behind me, there was a tap on the window. I turned and saw my brother's shirtless profile in the glass, his acne-pocked face grinning.

Pussy, he mouthed slowly, and then wiggled his tongue.

*

"Dad, did you ever take things from enemy soldiers in Vietnam?"

"Things like what?"

"Like teeth or something. Or ears."

"That's in the movies," my mom said, scraping her fork against her plate. Through the kitchen window, a tugboat bellowed on the river.

"It was in *Universal Solider*," my brother said. "Dolph Lundgren takes the ears from a whole village before he and Van Damme shoot each other."

"Your father was in Army Intelligence," my mom said, glaring at Ben. "He never killed anybody."

"He killed a cow," my brother said.

"I did," my dad said to my mom, "and we ate it." He drank a slow sip of wine. My mom sat still, and we all listened to my brother chew his dinner.

"Where'd this come from, Lee?" Dad asked.

"This isn't dinner conversation," Mom said, glancing towards Dad, "and I'm quite glad your father only killed a cow."

We ate in silence for a minute.

"So did you?" I asked.

"Lee," Mom said.

"I bet lots of people did," my brother said, picking at an island-chain of blemishes on his cheek. "War is hell, man."

A look had slipped across my father's face that I couldn't quite read. He forced a smile at my brother.

"The Twins say an old vet from World War II keeps the head of a Japanese Solider at his house," I said.

"Sweet," my brother said.

Mom's eyed widened. "The Fogarty boys you play your little games with?"

"Your pussies and dragons games," my brother said.

"Benjamin that's enough."

"He lives next door to them and they mowed his lawn," I said. My father's caterpillar eyebrows were titled upward like a shrug, like an apology, but his face sagged at the jowls, and he let me finish.

" . . . So he invited them in afterward and showed it to them."

Out in the night-darkness it began to rain. The trees whispered and swayed, and a sweet, earthy smell drifted inside.

"I'd keep all the heads of my enemies," my brother said. He took his fingers and made an exaggerated air-quoting motion: "even the *cows*."

"That's it," my mother said, spreading her arms and pulling each of our plates away from us, "dinner is over."

My brother rolled his eyes and slid out of his chair, popping his knuckles loudly as he tromped upstairs. My father sat still, head bowed, and I hesitated at the table's edge.

"Dad?"

"You are dismissed, Lee," Mom said.

My father was running his tongue on the inside of his lower lip. He looked like he was on the verge of saying something, but each time his mouth opened he just took a breath, and after a while he gave me the same wry smile, his eyebrows up again, as if he were sorry for the words that only he could hear.

*

At D&D that week, nobody cared about the game except for Ernesto. When we arrived, The Twins presented us with a hand-drawn map of the old man's house, and each of us took a turn examining the layout as if we were studying the blueprints of a bank vault.

"It would be cool if he had the head booby-trapped," Marco said.

"He went downstairs and unlocked his basement to get it," Ricky said.

"And he brought it back down there after he showed us," Ronnie added.

Ernesto shuffled his papers behind the dungeon master's screen, and stacked the dice into columns on the table.

"You know, like Raiders of the Lost Ark," Marco said again, to nobody.

I looked at the paper map The Twins had made. One of them had taken the time to carefully label the rooms and draw the furniture they'd seen. There were dimensions written in both imperial and metric, and lots of little labels pointing to things like *stinky garbage can* and *leather recliner* and *Marine Corps flag on wall—red*. Ronnie—the more artistic twin—had drawn illustrations of muscular men in army gear shooting machine guns at one another crowded the margins. In one corner, a stack of egg-shaped ovals were drawn beneath a palm tree, each with a pair of x's for eyes, slashes for mouths, a splatter of crayon blood dotting their edges.

"What did the head really look like?" I asked them.

"Like a head," Ricky said, turning to Ronnie, who nodded.

"More like a skull," Ronnie added, "with some skin still on it maybe. He kept it in a nice wooden box."

"Like a mummy?" Ernesto asked. The Twins nodded.

The Twins' mom came in with grape sodas and we all made a half-hearted attempt to get down to business, but the game didn't go very smoothly. I could tell Ernesto was frustrated with us. He used more detail than usual, describing the gloom of the dungeon and the horrible stench that rose from the remains of adventurers who'd died in the catacombs of the Red Warlock. We were playing pirates, there to loot ancient treasure, but Ernesto seemed intent on denying us this prize. Every decision we made landed us in a trap or some unlikely turn of fate, and soon my Wizard had died from a well-placed javelin to the chest.

I left the others to soldier on while I wandered around The Twins' bedroom. To the left of the door were high windows that lit the walls with white, leaf-shadowed squares. Through one, I admired the other houses in the neighborhood. Each house was a mansion compared to where I lived, except for one at the end of the block: a squat, run-down camel-back shaded by a pecan tree. Black tar paper glistened where there were shingles missing, and I could see freshly-mown grass stretching along the streetside. I traced the map The Twins drew in my mind, turning my body one way and then another to orient myself, then checking out the window again. Ernesto watched me out of the corner of his eyes.

When my parents came to pick me up, I asked if we could give Ernesto a ride too. He lived in Black Pearl, and going there would take us past the house.

"I know what you're thinking," Ernesto whispered to me as we idled at the stop sign at the corner of the block. I ignored him and scanned along the grass-line of the house. My eyes came to rest on a small basement egress-window near the back yard. I stared hard at the glass, and the darkness beyond.

"I'm not going to help you," Ernesto said.

I glanced angrily at him. His deep brown irises were side-lit, his pupils shrunk to pinpoints.

"Saturday," I whispered back. "My parents will be out of town."

"It's not a game," he said. "It's a bad idea."

"Pussy," I said, blushing almost as soon as I said the word.

He blinked and looked away. My cheeks burned. I tried getting his attention again during the ride home, but his face remained expressionless, and when he exited the car, he didn't look back.

*

That night, I dreamt of dogs howling in a barn. The barn was on fire. Outside of the barn, men hung from live oak trees. The scene was grainy, sepia-toned, collaged together from images I'd seen in our social studies textbooks. Some men were stripped naked, the ragged contours of their anatomy approaching me in a slow zoom. A hand with two fingers missing. Sock-feet with no shoes. A string of intestines spooled out from a waistline, hanging past a black, pixelated gap where a penis should have been. Soon I was aware of other faces at the edge of the picture—ghosts with cameras, some of them smiling, some of them stern and featureless. I felt the heat of the fire, smelled my brother's sweat like pitch bubbling from burning pine.

I woke to rain in the trees, a late New Orleans lullaby, and then remembered nothing.

*

On Friday morning, my parents packed the minivan for my brother's wrestling tournament in Shreveport. This would be Ben's first match of the summer, and I could tell he was nervous because his eyes were all the way open at breakfast. He looked like he hadn't slept at all. He rubbed his forehead with dirt-clogged fingernails. His face was a single, pink eruption of acne.

After he ate, my brother excused himself while my parents loaded a cooler with bottles of Pedialyte and peanut butter sandwiches. They brought down suitcases that were packed like they were going on a cruise. Dad carried Ben's gym bag out last, holding it in front of him with a mix of revulsion and reverence. My brother had not washed his bag since he made varsity.

Mom kissed my forehead and reminded me that the babysitter wasn't going to cook for me or do any laundry, so I had to take care of myself. As she talked, I saw Layla walking on the far side of the street. There was no dog in front of her, and her arms were straight at her sides. She glanced at us but kept moving, one step after the other toward the end of the block and out of sight.

Finally my brother emerged—not from the house, but from the back yard with a tennis racket in his hand. The strings were covered in a thick orange pulp, the guts of buck moths that clouded the cypress trees in our alley. His half-lidded smile had returned, and he tapped the racket onto the driveway.

"Yuck," my father said.

"Doing you a service," my brother said. "Fewer caterpillars next year."

"Ben, say goodbye to your brother," Mom said.

My brother looked at me. For a moment, there was a wetness in his eyes that shimmered strangely. I would only recognize this much later in life, through the visiting glass at the penitentiary in St. Gabriel, for the look of desperation that it was. For now, we just took each other in, the mute exchange hanging in the air between us. Then he grinned and popped his knuckles at me, curling each finger down one at a time until only his middle finger remained.

*

The night had many voices. The pulsing scree of tree frogs. A train crossing the river on the Huey P. Long. The howl of dogs cascading through the neighborhood, one after another, relaying news of what passed in the dark. Even the stillness had a voice—the click of the AC, the creaking bones of our house settling inch by inch into the soil.

Tonight, these voices kept me restless. Nothing was sitting right. A dread had been percolating in my gut all evening, and now, as the shadows flicked across my bedroom wall, I rose and tiptoed to listen at the babysitter's door. Then I took the stairs silently, found my sneakers, and slipped out the back door. The night breathed wetly on my skin. Roaches scuttled along the bricks. Fog drifted through the yellow haze of streetlights.

As I stood on the path, I became aware of a rustling sound somewhere nearby. My heart quivered. I suddenly pictured Layla from earlier that afternoon, walking straight-backed on the far side of our street, still searching for her dog. I whistled softly, and the rustling stopped. I tiptoed past my mother's garden. Even in the dark, I was sure I could recognize that dog. It would be hungry. It would be glad to see a friendly face, or glad to be called and cooed the way I'd seen Layla do so many times from afar. I wished I'd grabbed something to eat from the kitchen, but there was no time to turn back. The rustling started up again, and I followed it around my father's canoes, towards a narrow strip of ground hidden on the far side of the shed.

Here girl, I whispered, *it's ok girl, it's ok.*

A low growl rose from behind the shed. I stepped back, and street lamps lit the ground ahead of me. Two white eyes bobbed in the shadows. A black-ringed tail swung round, and a large raccoon scuttled away through the cypress duff. It climbed the alley fence, then paused to look back at me. Where it had been, a fresh mound of earth rose above the leaf litter. Someone had dug and re-filled a hole here recently. The raccoon had tunneled six or seven inches down on one side, and there at the bottom, a tiny, mangled paw protruded from the ground, its black-matted fur hanging in ribbons. The raccoon let out a hiss, flashed its ghost eyes, then vanished.

*

My legs moved and I followed them. There was a sound in my head like rain on the roof at night. All I knew was that I needed to go. I passed Ernesto's house, then Layla's, but I didn't stop. I tried to imagine knocking on Layla's door, but I couldn't picture the rest—what I'd say, who I'd say it to, what could possibly come after. Instead, I saw shapes twisting in the trees, pushing up through the soil below me. My brother emerging from the back yard earlier that afternoon. The roar grew louder.

For an hour, I passed through a midnight tunnel of live oaks and ivy-tangled fences. Occasionally, a pair of headlights swept by. I wore the night air around me like a cloak. No twig broke beneath my feet; no acorn popped against the buckling sidewalk. The moon drifted free of the clouds overhead. Eventually, the corner of The Twins' block came into view. Wind stirred the branches. I tasted the air, and swallowed the darkness.

When a car finally rattled over the pothole at the intersection, I punched a stone through the old man's low basement window. The window frame was narrow, but still wide enough for me to slip through. The basement smelled of mold and paint thinner. The concrete floor was slick beneath my feet. I crept forward blindly, my outstretched hands coming to rest against the smooth face of a door. It caught on a lock when I tired the handle. Closing my eyes, I pictured The Twins' map in my head: their guess at the layout of the house, the door they'd described at the bottom of the stairs.

I traced my steps back, and emerged from a hallway to find I could now see a little more clearly. Shapes emerged from the gloom. A hot water heater. A hanging tool rack. Tall metal grids of shelving. And there, on a short-legged table in one corner, was a box. It was the right size, only a little larger than a shoebox, polished and smooth to the touch. I didn't even think about it. Blood was now roaring in my ears. The box went out through the window, and then I did too. Glass teeth bit my skin, but I didn't care. Above me the floorboards creaked, and once outside I could see a light was switched on. The old man may have woken for a glass of water. Maybe he heard a sound, or was hungry, or simply stared at himself in the mirror for a while, wondering if he'd fully woken from his dreams. Maybe, like a twin, he'd sensed that something had gone missing, but if he spoke, neither I nor the head would ever hear his words.

*

I never told Layla about the dog I'd found buried in our backyard. I never told anyone. Ben wasn't arrested until he'd dropped out of college a few years later. The detectives and counselors who interviewed my parents suggested that some people like Ben started out hurting animals first, that there were warning signs that maybe they'd missed. My parents grappled with this for a while. They'd close in on me, sifting through my room when I wasn't home, calling other parents when I slept over somewhere, whispering to each other in the kitchen when they thought I was sleeping.

I grappled with it too. One evening, not long after the wrestling trip, I almost told my father about what was buried behind the shed. Ben was at practice, Mom was at rehearsal, and Dad was alone in the kitchen, reading on the couch overlooking the back garden. He patted my hair without looking up from his book when I sat down. Crickets sawed in the dark. I sat picking at the scabs from the old man's window, waiting for the words to come, until there was nothing left but the warmth of my father's hand on my head and the stillness we kept.

*

In the story I let myself tell, I carried the box all the way to the river that night.

Above the levee ridge, the horizon glowed pink from refinery towers. Upriver to my right were the old plantation homes, their grounds now whitewashed into hospices and museums, their graves now quiet, their stately oaks lit with lanterns visible from the road. Downriver, tangled stands of willow stretched out into the floodplain along the inner curve of the Mississippi. Above the waterline, their boughs were draped with brightly-colored trash like drowned Christmas trees.

I crested the hill and came down through a gap in the foliage to the water's edge. There, I waded in until I was ankle-deep. The Mississippi pulled at me, gurgling in the dark. The skin on my arms went prickly, and the polished wooden box glowed in the moonlight. I tiptoed further out into the arms of the river. The box began to slip from my hands, and for a moment, I imagined how easy it would be to let my body be sucked away with it. Together, we would drift out into the center channel, past the frothing wake of tankers and the black-limbed logs washed down from Iowa and Nebraska and Wisconsin. We would float under stars that never set, until we passed over the lip of the land and into a trackless sea. When the sun finally rose, there would be nothing left of us to find.

In the other story, I stood in the water until the moon dipped low and the sky to the west began to lighten. Then I opened the box and looked.

The Known Unknowns

1.

What do we know about her, a retired social worker, wife to a stubborn sonofabitch who refused to evacuate when the big one finally came? What does it say about the sonofabitch that he teaches conservation law, that his eyebrows go untrimmed, that he jogs in Day-Glo short-shorts each evening along the flooded path of the streetcar line? What did it mean when he struck his youngest with an open palm that same sweltering summer, when he tucked the boy into bed later that night in his softest hand-me-down shirt—the one from the marathon where he blew his knee out—and then sat cross-legged in a chair in the hallway, his fingers working little chunks of paper from the pages of his book until the boy was asleep? What does she say to him when they speak to each other in French, their voices tense but volume-capped somewhere just below shouting, each with one eye on the children wheeling their plastic dump trucks in the garden? What words does she recite when the sun sets and he still hasn't returned from canoeing in the swamp, when she knows he purposely tries to get lost, just a little more earnestly each year, even as his body thins out, dries up, crackles like tinder when he walks? What kind of love knows that he truly lives to be alone?

2.

We might think she's chosen to be the stitches for a man bent on unraveling. We might make easy metaphors about a city and its people, each duty-bound by momentum to raise the stilts and keep going. Some questions likely don't have an answer beyond the fact that he suspects, in ways he wouldn't articulate to himself, that he is himself still a child, that striking his boy proves he will always be one, and although this suspicion is a source of dread for him, it is also a strange and bitter reassurance. He likes, for instance, that they'd made a game of speaking French to each other around the kids, taking something originally meant to hide their fights and using it to talk about the things they'd otherwise lost the words to say. And when he's gone, alone in the woods or the swamp, no calls past dark and the empty driveway visible through the open front door, she will say a few of those words like a chant over a mug of tea. For her kind of love is only sentimental at the surface—hand-holding after dinner, a weekly picnic on the river levee when summer heat gives way to fall. The core of her love is pragmatism. Let it be quick, she'll say to the tea. Let it be quick, and let him be alone.

3.

Tomorrow New Orleans will bulldoze one hundred vacant homes. Three people will be shot, and a car fire at the I-10 onramp will stop traffic from mid-city all the way uptown, a line of honking cars that he will bike past on his way to work, still sleepy from making it home late, his mind still on the blackness of the water at sunset, the canoe still atop their battered station wagon, duckweed and a film of sulfurous mud still caked to his shins. She will walk the dog, past the neighborhood trees that survived the storm, past the toy figurines from her sons' toy chest that she's left in their branches as talismans, and home again to their sun-washed kitchen for tea, a check of weather, and a long, unquiet silence.

Save Point

The dream first appeared to him on a canoeing trip in the high desert of Oregon. It came to him in the tent, in the afterglow of adrenaline from a spill he and his father had taken in a rapid. They'd run it because they couldn't line it, a rapid that swept around a steep basalt curve, the green boiling water cutting deep under the cliffs and sweeping over a staircase falls. There were no shallows to wade the boat through safely. There were no tracks over the ridge, no portage that might allow them to jump a few hundred yards downstream and put back in the river. His father had grinned at him as they scouted the upstream approaches, knee-deep in the shallows and peering around the curve.

"Only one way to go," his father had said, his voice half-drowned in the echo of the falls around the bend. The boy had felt the tug of the water along his legs. High above them a pair of turkey vultures wheeled lazily in the darkening sky. The sun had dipped beyond the far canyon wall, and the air had taken on the coolness of the rock—wet and clammy and densely cold.

Afterward, in the tent, the boy stripped to the skin and pulled on his polypropylene long johns from the dry bag. He then cocooned himself in his sleeping bag, watching his father through the screen of the tent. His father was standing naked by the fire, tending to makeshift laundry lines he'd strung between paddles jammed vertically into the sand. On the lines hung their jackets and socks, baking in the smoke. The fabric would be peppered with tiny burn holes from the sparks. His father's skin was painted orange and red, his face pitted with shadows, his thin white hair a dandelion in the wind. The light danced on the canyon walls. The boy closed his eyes.

In his dream he was at the head of the rapid again, steadying the canoe as his father nosed the bow into the current. There was a fuzziness to the picture, a tippyness in the water that felt magnified, and the boy found himself watching the two approaches, inside and outside, knowing what had happened earlier, knowing that they were about to take the outside and flip, knowing that they'd catch a rock broadside halfway down and buckle into the water. He felt the stroke of his father's paddle press them to the outside approach and he heard a voice. *Here*, it said, and the world slowed to a halt, the roar falling quiet as night snow. The water beneath his boat was held rigid, the air became a deep breath clutched in his chest. He looked left, then right.

*

The save points came anachronistically, he learned. They offered themselves up in his dreams, spottily here and there, with no seeming order or consistency to the events that produced them. He'd lie in his bed and they would develop as a memory within a dream, blooming amidst an ordinary recollection of the past day's events. On the camping trip, and several times after that, he'd felt these dreams were different but he hadn't known what they meant. He'd taken that step back in time, hovering at some moment now hours gone, and the voice—his voice, he learned—would offer him the choice. *Here*, it would say, and the world would freeze at the precipice of several options. Before he knew how to use them, in those early dreams, he'd look at the memory like a painting, scrolling his gaze around the edges to the details he hadn't noticed the first time through. There had been a prairie falcon perched on a branch along the canyon walls by that rapid. Later, beyond the open door of his brother's car, there had been a thin stalk of lightning etched in a cloud beyond the city's skyline. He could inspect the brushwork of these scenes. He could zoom in and out, leap back into the void and then swing low across the landscape like a bird of prey. Then he'd return to where he'd been when the scene had paused. He'd do nothing, waiting for the sound and the motion to return. Eventually, time would start again, the memory would continue, and he would wake up.

*

On Christmas Eve, he tried something different. The dream that night was of the walk he and his father had taken in the woods that afternoon, a gray and rainy day where the fog drifted in off the Mississippi River and hung between the bare trunks of trees with a stink of brine and diesel. They'd had his father's ancient dog,

Loki, along with them. She was a mutt with shaggy black hair and stubby legs and a face like a little black bear, and she was always game for these walks. She'd bounded ahead along the trails off-leash while the boy and his father talked. They noticed after a while that the dog hadn't come back around—their *Heyyy Loki!* and *Come on girl!* dissolving flatly in the wet air around them. The woods weren't deep. They were flanked by the river on one side and the access road on the other, so they fanned out and started a sweep, calling her name, clapping and shouting, feeling a panic start to rise as they peered into tangled thickets, into sinkholes, underneath rafts of detritus washed into the underbrush.

When darkness fell, the boy left his father on the edge of the woods and ran home to get flashlights. On the way, he'd pictured how his mother would react. He pictured how the light within the warm walls of his house would extinguish at the loss, how the holiday would become a perfunctory exercise, a ritual of self-comfort instead of celebration, a wake for wayward Loki. And then, when he'd arrived at home, there she was, bedraggled and wriggling in his mother's arms. It turned out she'd gotten lost and just taken off for home. She'd crossed the access road, the highway traffic, navigated the neighborhood on her own and just showed up on their front porch, barking.

His mother had sent him back with flashlights, and his father cried when he found him there, still searching in the night woods. They made it to the late church service, and the four of them sat shoulder to shoulder in the pew. His brother prayed aloud when it was time. His mother kept an arm across each of their shoulders, smiling in the candlelight while the choir sang Silent Night. Around him he'd felt warmth and gratitude, the thankfulness of this near-miss, but his father remained shaken. When the lights came up, he saw his father's face was pale. His eyes had remained elsewhere during the service, his lips moving absently to the words and prayers and benediction.

When the dream came that night, the world had frozen at the point he and his father were walking out the door, heading for the river woods. He looked at the dog, locked utterly still in mid-approach to the door. On impulse, he reached out and shut the door. There was a strange rush, and the fabric of the world seemed to invert itself, like a coat worn inside-out. The saga of Loki's near loss, the search in the woods and the miraculous Christmas journey home, became a dream he'd had. The true history of Christmas Eve became a story in which they'd left Loki at home, barking in the yard while mother cooked the soup. In this story, the walk in the woods led to a conversation about politics, a sharing of his father's memories in the Korean War. In this story, his father's face stayed bright at the church service—the early one—and he sang loudly, making intentional goofs to the words of hymns, taking nickel bets with the boy and his brother about what time the service would conclude.

In the morning, they ate pancakes and unwrapped presents in the kitchen. The boy dropped pancake pieces to Loki, who scuttled happily amidst shards of tape and paper. His mother scolded him, and Loki licked her chops, her muzzle pressed against his leg. He felt the strangest sensation as she did this. Later, by the fire, he thought about telling his father that he'd had a dream where Loki had gotten lost, where they'd assumed she'd fallen in the river, been hit by a car, been swallowed up by the night fog. But the words didn't come. Instead, he held his tea until the hot ceramic mug scalded his palm, puffing steam across the room and wondering what else he could change.

*

As he came to recognize the dreams when they appeared, he began to change them more and more. Doing this didn't mean that the opportunities would happen more often, however. There remained an indecipherable pattern, a sense of capriciousness to when these dreams would occur. And yet he came to desire them. He came to recognize their texture, to feel a thrill that almost jolted him awake when he watched, while sleeping, a memory slow down and condense into a still-life picture. *Will this be the night,* he would wonder, after a fight with a girlfriend or a poorly-taken test. He imagined them as God pressing pause, saving his progress just in case. He started playing games with himself, predicting where a save point might be, when he might get a second go at something.

By his final year of college, his friends began to drift away from him, less out of a recognition of his strangeness than because his attention always seemed to be somewhere else. One by one, they gave up trying to extract a conversation out of him. One by one, they began to fill their plans with other people, began to regard him as an acquaintance whose path had veered sharply away from their own. He became a lost sailor in an ocean without harbors. They watched him move his lips when he thought no one was looking. *Here*, he would say to himself, as he walked around in the daytime, *here here here*.

*

When the accident happened, his brother hadn't been driving. The driver—a guy who shot pool with a cue that unscrewed in the middle and came in a shiny leather case—convinced his brother that he wasn't sober enough to get them home, which was true. The driver had been following the rules too; it was the other car that blew a stop sign and T-boned theirs. The driver was killed on impact. The boy's brother had been pressed into the crumpled metal of the door, the passenger side of the car wedged against a bank of parking meters at the corner of the intersection. His legs had been crushed but he was alive and talking when they cut him out of the car, mumbling the names of his family and bobbing his head between the slick of oil on the pavement and the hushed sky.

The boy had actually seen his brother several hours earlier. They'd met for dinner at their parents' house, and each was heading out for the evening afterwards. They'd spoken about meeting up for a movie. The boy's mind had been on a girl, and he'd not really listened to what his brother had been saying before he drove off to the pool hall. It had rained in the early evening, and a late summer squall had been building over the suburbs out west. The sky was dense, the wind edgy, the clouds a deep pink from the lights of downtown. He'd hugged his brother briefly, and then let him go.

They stayed that night at the hospital, on cots provided by the ER staff in an empty corner of the waiting room. His father and mother lay in each other's arms beneath a thin blue microfiber blanket. He watched the fabric heave with their breath in the ozone light. His eyes were dried at the edges, his hands tucked around his body and hugging himself as he sat Indian-legged on his cot, nodding in a slow rhythm. Names and codes squawked over the PA. Doctors came and went. Eventually a surgeon appeared with a nurse. His brother was stable. His parents sobbed, held each other, held him. His brother would likely lose his legs.

They held tighter. But he would live.

Later, when the first pinks and golds of dawn began to creep through the windows of the waiting room, his parents slept. He looked at his pillow, at the thin blue blanket he would wrap himself in, and his heart fluttered. He willed his eyes shut. He willed it with a strength so deep that he felt his guts twisting with the effort. But sleep, and the dream, would not come. He rubbed his eyes and watched the stars explode against the backs of his eyelids. He spoke the words, a chant in the quiet hum of the hospital, and pictured crawling out of the emergency room in his mind, back through the evening, back to the movie he'd seen without his brother, back to the front yard, under the deep pink clouds that rolled above the trees, back to where he stood in the wet grass in a brief embrace. To the smell of his brother's jacket. To the dinging of the keys in the ignition. Heat lighting flickered, tugboats moaned along the river. Cicadas sang in the trees. He kept rewinding, again and again. He watched the underbelly of those clouds, the underside of an uncurling wave, and waited for the leading edge to drift slowly, mercifully, to a stop.

What Distant Deeps

The man was lying on a log when the trapper found him. He'd taken off his rain slicker and reversed it so the bright orange lining faced outward, spreading it across a tangle of branches before laying each of his socks out to dry. From the woods, it had appeared to the man that the log bridged the bayou completely, but once on it, he saw the top third had been shorn off when it fell. All the trees in this part of the swamp were like this. They crisscrossed the waterways like fallen Roman columns, their dry sides spotted with turtles that basked in the late spring sunshine. The treetops in the forest were ground off in a line, cracked and bent and draped in the foliage of their neighbors, their trunks all tilted at a soft angle towards the southwest. The undergrowth was also treacherous now, as if a great broom had swept up the entire delta into the trees and encased it there in a gray coat of mud. Channels and canals the man had once known were now choked with deadfall, a maze of cutoffs and dead ends. When the man had reached the cypress trunk he now lay upon, he'd stopped a while to smoke a cigarette, straddling the log, the rubber tips of his boots tracing tiny arcs in the water. A jet trail dissolved in the wind high above him. A tidal breeze rose and fell in the branches. Below him, the cypress descended beneath the surface like the prow of a ship, the bark along the hull turning yellow and then coffee-brown before disappearing in the gloom.

"Where's your boat," said the trapper. His voice was squeezed with a wet gargle in the vowels. His sun-browned face had a sheen to it, less like sweat than a waxy coating that polished over a deep latticework of wrinkles. The architecture of his bones was birdlike, the man thought. A beak nose, high cheeks, a loose neck wattle that tensed with the quick movements of his jaw.

"No boat," the man said slowly. He watched the trapper approach, his trawling motor cocked at a 45 degree angle so that the flatboat drifted noiselessly along the water. The hull bumped the edge of the log with a soft boom, spinning a leisurely turn into the bank and scraping the chokeberry along the metal gunwales.

"No boat," the trapper repeated dubiously. "Where's your weapon?

"I'm not hunting," the man said. He was now sitting up on the log, the right side of his face feeling sunburned. The trapper sat still in his boat.

"No boat and no weapon," said the trapper. "What you out here for?"

"Looking for a bird."

The trapper scowled. "You ain't DNR are you?"

"No." The man lifted the rain slicker off the branches and showed the trapper the outside breast pockets. No logos, no badges. "Are you?"

The trapper spat with a smooth turn of his torso, his eyes squinting. Behind him in the boat, coils of thick filament line lay atop a rough stack of cages, every surface spotted Day-Glo green with algae and duckweed.

"Are you fucking with me?" he said.

*

April had been a hot month in southern Louisiana. In Lafayette, the sweet olive had begun to bloom early, blanketing the streets with a rotting sweetness. Cockroaches ventured along the cracks in the sidewalks and hovered in high corners. Whistling ducks coasted the thermals in the pink-clouded night, their calls waxing and waning northward and away towards red-clay woods and the Ozark folds. Moths clouded streetlights and the red-lit towers of marsh refineries. Fires burned dead foliage. Along the southeastward curve of the Mississippi River, in the wreckage of New Orleans, bodies were still occasionally revealing themselves. Their numbers had declined steadily since December, clusters of five and ten dwindling to single cases emerging from the earth. Here, one pressed into the storm drain beneath the concrete loops of Interstate 10. There, one bound up in trash and underbrush at the high tide line, its flesh picked over but still marked by flashes of color: an orange sock, a belt buckle, a thin gold chain that shimmered through the weeds on sunny afternoons. At night the marshland hummed in the wind, the grass parted by empty footsteps.

*

The man's father had been a hunter. There had been a camp out on the edge of the Pearl River Swamp, where as a boy he knew summers as a light in the trees, fire sparks in the yard at night, the smell of meat from the walk-in cooler and the smoking shed. There were mornings of birdsong and night choruses of cicadas. The boy had loved the birds. He found himself chattering their conversations as he stomped about the trails, warbling and cooing and clucking. He never felt he'd got the sound quite right, but he was a careful student of his father's birdcalls. In particular, he'd loved the wavering moan his father made through a blunted wooden flute during duck season. He would crouch behind his father in the shadow of their blind, holding his breath and watching the glint of twilight on the gunmetal and the polished woodgrain stock. In those moments, he sometimes thought about what the ducks would hear as they coasted in lazy circles towards a clearing in the woods, about what appeals and promises were made in the voice of that flute.

At night, he would walk the treeline of the camp, moving through the high grass at the edge of the clearing where the pine and tupelo gums sprang up. Some nights, orange firelight from the pit danced on the wet boughs. When his father expected visitors at the camp, the floodlights would be on, widening the visible world into tall shadows and white silhouettes. Other nights, the light was just a thin, staccato blue from the bug zapper over the porch, arcing with an electric hiss now and then, the flash echoing off into the air like heat lightning. He used to imagine, on nights like these, that he heard some throaty call from the woods. Sometimes it was a moan. Sometimes it was a whisper against the tapestry of night-noise, some uncanny approximation of a voice in the trees. It spoke in half-words, asking him to step out of the light and come find it. He'd play a game with himself, standing at the rim of the clearing and staring into the dark, counting as high as he could go before finally turning to run.

*

They sat together, the man and the trapper, in a patch of sun on the bank. The man ate a peanut butter sandwich from his bag. He chewed slowly and watched the trapper's hands. Long brown fingers worked on a knot that anchored a Styrofoam buoy the size of a softball to a rusted metal trap in the bow of his boat. After a few minutes, the trapper stopped and reached into the boat for a polished flask. He handed it to the man without a word and went back to his knots.

From the woods across the bayou a pair of shots crackled in the distance. A great blue heron emerged from the wake of a downed tree and skipped along the water, its wings beating heavy strokes until it rounded a bend in the channel. The man watched the muscles in the shoulders of the bird flex and pull. He took a drink from the flask and closed his eyes.

"That your bird?" the trapper asked.

The man shook his head slowly, eyes still shut. The trapper spat again, and the heat settled down on top of them as the breeze died.

"You lose your boat out here?" the trapper said.

"Gave it away," the man replied.

"Broke?"

"No it worked fine."

Above them the wind rose in the branches. Seed pods from the canopy of maple trees twirled in helicopter arcs, tic-tacking against the dead leaves as they landed.

"What's the sense in giving away a workin' boat?" the trapper asked.

The man didn't answer right away. He watched water bugs skip along the surface of the bayou, flicking around the edge of the boat to where the butt of a twelve-gauge shotgun protruded from a canvas carry bag. He chewed a while before speaking.

"Cops needed it."

"Ain't no cops around here taking nobody's boat."

"A while back. In New Orleans."

The trapper didn't look up but his fingers slowed, then stopped, like gears winding down on a clock. "Yeah?"

"Yeah."

The man watched the trapper pull the line taut, cinching the knot tight against the lip of a cage, then letting the whole thing clatter against the bottom of his boat. Little earthquake ripples spread across the water from the hull, overtaking the water bugs and tossing them, sending them dancing into the sunlit expanse.

*

Bennett Charbonnet had once taught the man how to make traps when they were boys. Bennett was held back in school and was twice the other boy's size by sixth grade, a body racing to maturity with a soft face that wobbled when he ran and flushed rosy and white in the wintertime. They'd prowled the pinewoods up by Picayune on bicycles together, washing the red-rust mud out of their gears with a garden hose at his grandmother's house. Bennett had an army survival manual that his dad had given him, a beige paperback with bloc-print letters and numbers stamped across the top of the front cover. It was pre-Vietnam issue, covering survival in all conditions and climates and the general cannon of self-reliance in the wilderness. There were crude drawings of toxic plants, of men using their pants for floatation when their boat sank. There were schematics for a lean-to, for braiding vines and tree fibers into cording, for accounting for latitude and navigating by the stars. The chapter Bennett dog-eared that summer was all about traps—deadfalls and tripwires, noose-snares and improvised fish corrals that looked like stick castles at the edge of a stream.

For all their efforts that summer, the boys had caught a total of two ground squirrels. Both had been with the noose-snare and figure-four trigger device. The hardest part of the figure-four was getting the trigger pin—just a stick about three inches long—to fit well enough into a notch so that it held the tension of a sapling bent over on itself next to the trail. Because Bennett was a quicker study with such things, the boy held the line from the end of the bent sapling while Bennett fastened the trigger pin into the frame of the trap. Afterward, they would pile up the underbrush along the trail until it narrowed to the width of the noose they'd dangled. The boy enjoyed this part, making a funnel of stones and twigs that herded the prey into the middle of the trail, forcing it to choose whether it wanted to abandon the route it knew or risk passing through the noose.

"We can make a man-sized snare if we can find a big enough sapling to bend," Bennett said one afternoon, admiring one of their squirrels as it dangled from a line several feet above their heads.

"Ain't no man going to get caught in a snare trap," the boy replied.

"Ain't for no man anyhow," Bennett said.

Bennett had been checking out books from the public Library in Picayune about Native American cultures for a class project, and had become obsessed with a creature called the "Letiche." Creoles called it the Kietre, a kind of bigfoot of the swamp, all shag hair and taller than any man, with eyes that glowed yellow like lanterns in the dark. They'd played in the mud of Bennett's driveway once, using the soles of their sneakers to carve out the approximate shape of the Letiche's footprint. Bennett measured the length on hands and knees, sculpting the angle of the toes with his fingers. On the nights at the edge of the clearing by his father's camp, the boy had often watched the winking of fireflies in the woods and imagined the drifting gaze of a monster in the dark. It spoke to him there in whispers. He would clench his fists. And then he would count and count and count.

*

The man had known things would be bad at his father's camp. He had steeled himself for it. In the long months of fall and winter, while the drowned city was still closed, he'd spent his nights lying on his back in a Motor Inn in Baton Rouge, waiting and thinking. He could still remember the orange light from the parking lot of that hotel, light that cut through the window where his shades didn't reach. It cut a stripe down the television set, skirted the dusty painting of a fisherman and ran along the spackled ridges of the plaster ceiling. He'd lay there on the outside of the bedspread in his underwear, too hot to sleep, following that line with his eyes. Some nights he'd thought about his apartment complex back in New Orleans. Some nights he'd tried calling his family: his retired uncle out in New Mexico, his cousin who taught kindergarten in Tampa. Most nights he'd just lay there, listening to the clicking of the AC unit underneath the window, the shouts from the street outside, the night traffic roar from I-10—and he'd think about the camp.

Even before he'd gone back into the city for the search and rescue, when the National Guard had put a call out to anyone with a boat to come down and join the effort, he'd known things would be just as bad up here. The eyewall of Katrina had skipped east of New Orleans in the final hours before landfall, taking out the casinos along the shores of Mississippi, boiling and swelling the gulf twenty feet high before rolling through Lake Borgne and the Pearl River Swamp under the cover of darkness. It had scoured this land of the trees and houses and all the creatures too slow or too stubborn to avoid its coming. He had seen the city to which the storm had delivered a glancing blow. He knew without knowing to expect the worst.

But all his anticipation, all the preparation and hardened nerves, had been ambushed in the blue light of this morning. He'd felt a shift of gravity, an ever-unfolding sense of dread as he followed highway 90 east across the state line. Knowing that the nearby town of Pearlington had been wiped out wasn't the same thing as seeing it. There were downed streetlights and houses collapsed off their foundations, but mostly, there was just nothing. Up the 604 near his turnoff, a double-wide had been pressed into a stand of pine trees, a sign spray-painted in orange letters along its side that said *Doyle is Staying*. The squeak of his brakes echoed in the ruins. When he'd found the lane to the camp, he'd had to tow deadfall out of the way several times with his pickup's winch. Each time he got out to hook the tow line, his vision spun.

By the time he'd reached the camp, he felt too dizzy to get out again. He switched off the ignition and just looked. There ahead of him was the silhouette, the first yellow glint of morning tracing the upper edges of the eaves, but the shape was all wrong. The roof of the porch had been flipped downward like a garage door, the support beams buckled and splintered in the high grass. The body of a tupelo gum lay embedded in the east wall by the kitchen, and around its gnarled branches the roof had sagged inward. The shingles were mostly gone, and the tarpaper glistened with dew. A family of grackles fluttered from an empty window frame. He closed his eyes. He kept them closed, and when he opened them again the full light and fire of southern April sunshine was scorching the world.

*

"My father told me he heard a bird out here once," the man said. A calm had settled on the bank where they lay, and the trapper's boat rested serenely in the slack eddy of the fallen cypress log. Even the bugs seemed to still themselves, as if this hour of the afternoon had been scheduled for a deep breath. "It was this woodpecker that was supposed to be extinct."

The trapper eyed him and tested the weight of his fuel can. "That the bird you come out here for?" he said.

"Maybe," the man said. "But no, I don't think there's any finding this bird." He paused for a second, as if saying the words had been the first time he'd considered them. He looked over his shoulder into the trees. "I really came out to see my dad's old hunting camp. He passed a few months before the storm last year, and I hadn't gotten out here to see it before now."

The trapper dug into his boat with sinewed arms, coming up with a small wire cage.

"I check these lines at night sometimes," the trapper said. "Got to use a spotlight to catch the gator eyes in the water, otherwise you go reaching in the wrong place and lose an arm."

The man nodded, sweat beading on his upper lip.

"I come up one night and see them eyes by my buoy," the trapper says. "I keep the light just so I can see him, but he just sits there for a while. No hurrying him, so I wait and he wait."

"He ever let you check the trap?" the man asked.

"After a while, he blinked and went under," the trapper said. "But before I paddle over, he come up again to watch me, and I couldn't believe it. He was whiter than the moonlight on water. Four foot maybe, but white as sugar."

The man waited, but the trapper just held the cage in the air.

"I saw an albino gator in the zoo back in New Orleans once," the man said. "They've got him in a tank all on his own."

The trapper shook his head. His thin eyes had opened just a little, etched in shadow beneath his brow.

"Weren't no albino," the trapper said. "This one was different."

The man watched the trapper's face and let his words settle. "I just remember thinking it was a shame how they had him separated like that," he said. "Last thing you see before the toilets and the parking lot."

The trapper seemed to think about this. He cracked a grim smile, then glanced upwards. The sky had deepened to a cobalt blue, the sunshine shifting further west now and angling through the tree branches. To the south towards the gulf, distant white towers of thunderheads boiled in the haze, their uppermost plumes tinged with crimson. Long shadows had begun to creep across the water.

"S'pose you'll want a ride back to that camp of yours," the trapper said.

*

When the man slept, he dreamed of birds. A dream he'd had several nights before he decided to drive out to the camp: He was standing in a taxidermy shop with his father. A gallery of animal heads watched them as they talked. His father was saying something important about the ivory bill—he felt the sense that this was so—but he could not pull his gaze away from the animals on the wall. Their heads were strange combinations of familiar creatures—a nutria with feather plumage, a jackrabbit with deer antlers jutting from its forehead. It seemed they muttered as his father spoke, clouding his words. He heard his father say, "They're the only birds that do this. Three loud knocks, slow and steady." He heard the knocks, but when he turned to look, his father was gone.

*

When he lay awake at night, the man would remember the boats. In the boats, there had usually been a guardsman and a cop to ride along. The guardsmen were mostly young, maybe half his age. The cops were older guys, unshaven and low on sleep; many didn't wear their uniforms after the first day. The cops came along because they knew the city layout. But the layout was hard to figure in the water. Most street signs in New Orleans were either already missing or laid in tile on the corners, and the black water reflected the buildings it had enveloped so perfectly that the man—who had known the city for much of his life—felt the whole place was otherworldly. They traveled along perfectly straight bayous, walled on either side with yellowing houses that jutted like ramshackle teeth upward and downward from the surface. Below and above them, the September sun scalded their arms, danced on their reflective glasses, skipped across the barrel of the guardsman's rifle.

On the fourth day in the boats, there wasn't any cop to ride along with them, so it was just the man and the guardsman. By now they'd settled into a routine, following a grid given to them by a Lieutenant who slept in the back seat of his Humvee. His guardsman that day was rotated in from another company, had been in the guard for eight years and had seen tours overseas. They made small talk and drank bottles of water that later rolled in the oily bilge at the bottom of the boat. That day they'd put in at the western edge of the lower ninth, motoring along St. Claude Avenue until the grid directed them northward at Charbonnet Street. The man had seen the sign in the water and felt a strange thrill at the name. He lowered the throttle and idled into the turn, coming so close to the green street sign that the top of the pole almost brushed against the edge of the hull. He watched the wake from the boat slide in viscous ripples along the surface, each collision with the wood veneer of the shops and houses nearby leaving a yellow stain of scrim along the waterline.

North of an elementary school, there had been a thin man on his 2nd floor balcony. The water lapped about six inches below the balcony, and a dog was poking its muzzle between the wrought iron balcony bars and the rain gutter, sniffing. The thin man was in an undershirt and jeans that had been cut above the knees, showing the angled ridge of his emaciated thighs. He had a large cooler and an umbrella duct-taped to the top of the balcony. The sunshine through the red fabric painted his glistening skin the color of arterial blood. Boats that had come this way earlier reported that he was here, but when they pleaded with him now he wouldn't leave his balcony. He asked them for water and they gave him all but two of their remaining bottles. The guardsman tried over and over to get the thin man into the boat, but eventually only convinced him to let them take the dog. Its black fur was hot to the touch, its lips foamy and its mouth hanging wide. As the dog worked to find its balance on one of the benches, the thin man on the porch pointed north.

"Some kids up that way," he said.

"Where?" the guardsman asked, "How do you know?"

"I hear they voices at night," the thin man replied. "I sleep out here."

"How many do you hear?" the guardsman asked.

The man followed the aim of the thin man's hand, followed the bony finger with his eyes towards where the water went deep until just the A-shaped peaks of houses broke the surface. Out here had been where the bodies were getting pulled from attics. Where rescue choppers had seen holes half-punched in the roofs. The dog whined and lapped at the bilge.

"Can't never tell," the thin man said. "But I hear em."

*

The ride out of the swamp was slow going. Each channel the trapper tried to take in the direction of the man's camp ran into an impassible wall of deadfall. After several attempts, the man told the trapper just to take him back to the road and he'd walk it from there.

"That'll be a big detour. You came further than you think," the trapper said. He pointed towards where the sun had dipped between the tree trunks. "That there's the west stretch of the Lower Black. If you're walkin' home from the road you'll be walkin' till morning."

"You spare the time to drive me up to Pearlington?" the man asked.

"I can take you as far as Nelta's," the trapper said. "Gotta get me some gas."

Around them the night was deepening. The mulch and sweet-earth and methane rot that clouded the afternoon air had given way to a breeze that brought salt in from the gulf. The darkness was growing up from the ground, climbing the knobbled cypress knees and filling the swamp. When the motor slowed, they could hear the roar of insects. They drifted across submerged limbs that bumped the bottom of the flatboat, their branches scraping along the metal like long, uncut fingernails.

*

As he helped the trapper load his boat onto the trailer, the man realized that he had actually been in a taxidermy shop once. He realized that his father had been there too, that he had taken him as a boy to get a red-breasted merganser stuffed after a hunting trip down in Plaquemines Parish. His father had still been wearing his winter marsh gear, topped with a blaze-orange cap pulled down low over his ruddy ears to the edge of where his beard bristled outward. The merganser he carried had a wild crown of green hair that swept back like a mohawk along the ridge of its skull. The boy waited while his father and the taxidermy man spoke. Then the taxidermy man went into the back room and returned with another bird, stuffed and mounted on a wooden plate. The bird was large, the size of a house cat, with a black and white striped face, a white throat set against black feathers, and a brilliant red crown. He leaned down to the boy, the smell of chewing tobacco tickling his face when the taxidermy man spoke.

"This here's the surviving king of the woodpeckers," the taxidermy man said, his lips wet and his eyes watching the boy. "Not an ivory bill, but the closest look you'll get at something like him."

The boy's father stood by and laid a hand on his shoulder. The boy touched the edge of the bird's cheek, clearing a small line of dust that dangled for a moment before falling. He tried seeing it alive in his mind, imagined the eyes wet, the feathers rippling with the graceful stretch of its wings. The eyes were black marbles, reflecting the overhead lights in semi circles. He could see the outline of his own face, bent in an oil drop. Then he touched his finger to an eye, gently, and the marble fell.

*

The only light in the trapper's truck came from the radio and cigarettes. The trapper and the man smoked in the cab, cigarette after cigarette. The man finished his pack and the trapper kept going, the breaks in the road clop-clopping beneath their tires and rattling the boat trailer behind them. The man realized that he'd been talking, was still talking, low at first, but still loud enough to hear his own voice over the road. The trapper made no sign that he noticed or was listening. The man watched clouds of bugs drift through the path of their headlights, feeling his mouth continue to move.

"It wasn't much of a boat really," he was saying, as if the volume had just come up on a record that had been playing for a long time. "Made for marsh fishing. The outboard was 20 horses and it probably held 350 pounds plus gear. The first time we took people out of a neighborhood we had to do it in shifts with another boat. We got a bigger lady in the bow and her neighbors started crying because they thought we weren't coming back for them. The cop volunteered to get out and wait, which was probably the right call because the water was at the gunnels the whole way home."

An empty shed at the roadside whipped by in the dark.

"We talked about it for a while, that guardsman and me, the last day in the ninth. The dog was throwing up from the bilge and the sun was cooking us, but the guardsman didn't want to give up. I'm ashamed I fought him on it. It was so hot that day."

Ahead in the dark, a lit sign poked through the trees, the only light they'd seen in miles. A fluorescent halo of gas pumps and a small, concrete bunker adorned with beer specials came into view. The truck angled in and slowed to a stop, but the trapper kept it running.

"We didn't find the kids," the man said. He opened his mouth to speak but nothing else came out. He swallowed and tried again. "We looked till nightfall. We just couldn't find them."

The trapper chewed grit in his teeth.

"I hope to God they were never there," the man said.

The trapper killed the engine and the cab went dark. The cab stayed dark when his door opened. He stepped out and then turned to face the man.

"I know about that bird you're lookin' for," he said. "The woodpecker. Older folks still talk about it. Say it was a beautiful thing." He paused. The man stayed silent.

"But you were right. Ain't no bird like that in these woods no more."

The man closed his eyes and leaned his head back against the seat.

"I'll take you the rest of the way," the trapper said. "Gonna piss and talk to Nelta. Stick around."

The trapper shut the door and walked across the lot to the gas station store. After a minute, the man saw him re-emerge through the glass doors carrying the key to the bathroom, trailing a large green squirt gun on a chain. When the trapper disappeared around the corner, the man got out of the truck, careful to keep the door from squeaking too loudly. He pulled his bag to his shoulders and walked across the concrete drive. Gravel and smears of gritty red clay crunched under his boots. He walked out from the beneath the overhead canopy, to the uncut grass already wet with dew, past ant piles, past the low dunes of road trash, over the knee-high metal rail, until he stopped. The wind rose. Warm night air ruffled his hair. It hissed in the high grass that now stood to the buckle of his jeans. He felt the bristle-tops of the grass through the denim on his legs, and he looked out into the forest. The gas station lights behind him strained to reach this far. His shadow stretched away in front of him like a long black road, up the trunk of the nearest tree and then was lost in the whispering dark. His legs twitched. He heard footsteps in the grass, imagined they were his own.

"Hello," he said to the night. And then he waited.

Last Match Fires

The sky is metal and gold behind ragged clouds. *Word of God type stuff,* he says, crouching on his knees. Beneath his hands are piles of tinder: crushed stalks of cheatgrass and pine needles, a bundle of dry twigs, the raw-paper insides of birch bark curled in white shavings on the ground. He bends over the piles while she watches. She holds his wool zip-up behind him, scoops out a shallow space of quiet air from the wind. She smells sage and the salt-hued musk of his body through his wet clothes. He crumples receipts from his pocket, dirt-fingers kneading and mincing the fibers. Then it's the matchbox, the deep breath, and a calm that holds the moment. Despite the cold, his hands don't shake. Her eyes drift upstream towards the place where the horizon splits, the light there pulsing like the afterglow of a camera flash, and she listens for the sound of the strike.

*

His charm is the charm of the lucky. She'd come to understand this once the seesaw cycle of their early years together had settled into a rhythm. They used to hitchhike together—leave the car by the riverside and then thumb their way back at the end of a long day of paddling. Once, coming off a canoe trip in western Mississippi, they stood in the twilight along a one-lane highway and flagged down a trucker who'd been just released from Angola for cutting his wife. Several years later, he talked a burglar out of their house in the middle of the night, laughing even as he did so, his smile hooded in moonshadow. They'd moved their stocks before the crash. They'd stayed through the storm but escaped New Orleans when the canal walls crumbled. She'd come to sense this pattern as a way of being, some deeper trust in the fabric of a world that ushered danger just beyond the borders of his path, but it was not an easy trust. She knew—or felt she knew—this light in his eyes as a foolish, fearless thing. She knew it as the purest detail of his person, the very thing that led him off to the backwoods without a map, to the courtroom without an appointment, to the roadside alone at twilight with his thumb splayed casually in the air. But it was a tiresome promise too. It whispered to her after each near-escape. In eddies of adrenaline, in the late hours, that eyelight became a reminder that nothing would ever quite be settled, nothing ever quite still.

*

Here, by the river, the tinder nest holds the flame. Wrinkles on his face deepen and stretch, his cheeks bright and dark again as he puffs air softly into the bundle. He piles sticks into a teepee and sings senseless words as if he were putting the fire to sleep. She settles down behind him, her arms around his midsection, feeling his breath vibrate through her skin. The wind turns and sparks scatter into the wool of his jacket. She looks back upriver to the horizon, past their overturned canoe hoisted into the junipers along the shore. The ridge is now black and backlit. Later, when their clothes are dry and a nightsong of insects closes in around them, she will dream and see his face once again by the fire, concentrating, poised to breathe into the tinder bundle. She will dream and she will see, for an instant that strays out of time, a strange recomposition, some terrible sadness like an oil drop slipping across his eyes, there and gone again, when the match strike burns to life.

Personal Thanks

This book stands on the shoulders of more folks than I can adequately thank here. My agent, Rachel Crawford, is a fantastic agent and wonderful person, and I'm lucky that she took a chance on me. I'm grateful to everyone at Orison—to Luke and Karen for their tireless efforts to bring these stories to life, and to David for his selection and celebration of this manuscript. I'm grateful to my faculty at the California Institute of the Arts and the Nonfiction Writing Program in Iowa: Tom Lutz, John D'Agata, Bonnie Sunstein, Robin Hemley, David Hamilton, Patricia Foster, and all of the stellar writers who shared those workshops with me.

I owe some, if not all, of this book to my dissertation committee at the University of Nebraska. To Joy Castro, for her compassion and stunningly-dedicated feedback—I wouldn't have even begun writing short stories without her. To Tim Schaffert, for his generosity as director of our Creative Writing Program, and to Ted Kooser, for his guidance and patience with a non-poet in his tutorial. To Dan Crawford, for his insights into faith and spirituality, and to Jonis Agee, without whom I and many other writers at UNL would have collapsed under the weight of the world.

I owe a significant debt to the editors and readers of the journals in which these stories first appeared, both for the publication and for the faith they've showed in my work. In particular, I'm grateful to Abigail Cloud at *Mid-American Review*, to Tim and Ruth and all the editors at *The Pinch*, Toni Graham at *Cimarron Review*, Adam Ross at *Sewanee Review*, Anna Schachner at *The Chattahoochee Review*, Justin and Alicia and the editors at *New Delta Review* for their kind nominations, and to Linda Swanson-Davies at *Glimmer Train* for selecting my story out of a very large pile.

I'm thankful for Jess Walter, Lance Cleland, Steve Yarbrough, Jill McCorkle, and all of the other folks at the Tin House and Sewanee workshops who have supported me. Thank you to TJ Fuller, Earl Marona, Robert Kerbeck and Robert Albrecht, Annabel Graham, Jill Koeningsdorf, Marie Stone, Colleen Busch, Janet Buttenweiser, and Michelle Lombardo. Thank you Matt Schmidt, David Armand, Paulette Boudreaux, Emma Burcart, Emily Choate, Jeff Condran, Denise Cline,

J. Edgar Blanton, Karin Davidson, Molly Dumbleton, Alina Grabowski, Karin Lin-Greenberg, Mary Sellers, Catherine Weingarten, Tara Weinstein, and Hillary Zaid. To my good friends, Adam Scheffler, Jordan Famer, Marcus Meade, Ryan Olberhelmen, Marty Chaffee, Casey Pycior, Wendy Oleson, Matthias Ziegler, Chris Bissonnette, and Hali Felt—you've all made this possible. There are many other talented, insightful, and good-hearted folks who I've doubtless omitted here, but for whom I am always grateful.

Lastly, my love and appreciation to Jess, Cyp, Bear, Arthur, Logan, Thibodeaux, Mom, and Dad: there is a little of you in everything I write.

About the Author

Gabriel Houck is originally from New Orleans, where his family still lives and in which many of the stories in *You or a Loved One* are set. Houck holds an MFA from the University of Iowa's Nonfiction Writing Program and a PhD in creative writing from the University of Nebraska–Lincoln, where he is currently a Lecturer in the English Department. His story "When the Time Came" was selected as a distinguished story in the 2015 edition of *The Best American Short Stories*, edited by T.C. Boyle, and other stories have appeared in *Glimmer Train, The Sewanee Review, Mid-American Review* (2014 Sherwood Anderson Fiction Prize), *Western Humanities Review, New Delta Review, Grist, PANK, Fourteen Hills, Bayou, Fiction Southeast, Sequestrum, The Cimarron Review,* and *The Pinch*, among other places.

About Orison Books

Orison Books is a 501(c)3 non-profit literary press focused on the life of the spirit from a broad and inclusive range of perspectives. We seek to publish books of exceptional poetry, fiction, and non-fiction from perspectives spanning the spectrum of spiritual and religious thought, ethnicity, gender identity, and sexual orientation.

As a non-profit literary press, Orison Books depends on the support of donors. To find out more about our mission and our books, or to make a donation, please visit www.orisonbooks.com.